Richard brought his free hand to her neck and stroked the backs of his fingers over her throat.

"Windermere," Esme whispered in an annoyed tone. "What do you think you're doing?"

"I think I'd like to make love to you, if you don't mind."

"I don't think that's wise," she warned, but didn't pull away.

"Don't make up your mind that you won't like something until you've at least tried it once." He laughed softly. "Isn't that what you told Lady Small to do earlier in the night?"

"Listening in?" she complained.

"I agree wholeheartedly." He'd never so much as kissed Esme before and he was desperate to taste her suddenly. Richard bowed his head slowly and set his lips to her neck. He nibbled her skin as she shuddered. "You don't have to say anything. Just let it happen."

HEATHER BOYD

REASON TO WED

Distinguished Rogues

7

Dedication

For John—a man who challenges me, loves me and sticks with me through thick and thin. You are the reason I write.
I love you so much.

Chapter One

Every woman can appreciate the challenge of making a man do what she wants. Unfortunately for Lady Heathcote, Esme to her closest friends, her chances of success tonight seemed to have fled along with her lover. "Now where has he gone?"

She scanned the room in search of Mr. Albert Meriwether. However, it was becoming increasingly clear that inviting him to Lord Windermere's house party in Gloucestershire had been a colossal mistake on her part. She had his attention here even less than she had in London, and no one had even been stolen from or murdered. She should have broken with him when she'd sensed his repeated reluctance to take time away from his important work in the city.

"He's across the room, making good on his intention to win every lord in attendance over to his cause," Lady Ames warned.

Again.

"I must say, if you had not mentioned your connection earlier today, I'd have had no idea you were such good friends," Lady Small whispered dramatically. "He's paid you less attention than our host and we all know you've been at odds with Windermere for an age."

Harriet met her gaze, her expression tinged with concern. "I've known of social climbers before of course, but never one so pointedly obvious as Meriwether."

"That wasn't why we came, Harriet," she complained softly to her friend and confidant.

Harriet squeezed her arm, full of sympathy. Esme had dragged Meriwether from London to reignite the spark of their affair before his obsession with his work snuffed it entirely. But he was determined to curry favor with the most influential lords in attendance. And if he couldn't gain their ears for long enough, he'd started being friendly toward their wives too.

She'd had more of his nonsense than she could tolerate, and turned away.

Esme left Harriet to her own devices and wandered the public rooms of Windermere Park on her own. The loveliest property she'd ever visited was home of the most arrogant man she'd ever met. She'd been surprised by the invitation to come this year, but never considered refusing after reading Windermere's most sincere apology for losing his temper with her. With his last lover, Lady Bartlett, being so proficient at amateur theatricals, it hadn't been surprising the woman had pulled the wool over his eyes, professing to a pregnancy that was just a myth. And it had been Esme's unfortunate sense of fair play that had prompted her to warn him that Lady Bartlett wasn't the least bit pregnant. His vitriol had fallen on her head-first, of course, but at least he'd listened and not married the devious woman.

In the hall, she encountered Windermere's ancient butler, a kindly soul who'd served the family forever. Oswin was a sweet old man who never failed to treat her well, so she stopped to speak to him when so many others wouldn't bother. "Good evening, Oswin."

He nodded. "Might I be of service, Lady Heathcote?"

She took in the lean to his posture and his tired expression and smiled. "Yes, you can go and sit down and let young Pip run around in your stead for the rest of tonight."

Pip was the newest footman employed here, but Esme was confident the young man wouldn't mind the extra work or the experience.

"It's my pleasure to serve the family," Oswin replied with his usual dignified loyalty.

"As you wish." She'd let the matter slide but privately thought a man his age should be already training his replacement. If she were mistress of this house, she'd have begun long ago. A long house party like this could send him to his bed from sheer exhaustion, and then where would the family be?

She glanced back inside the drawing room once more.

Lingering by the hearth, Meriwether laughed with Windermere's guests, most part of her extended circle of friends too. She considered each man in turn...their intelligence, their reputations. Their chances of being won over to Meriwether's cause to formalize protection for the wealthiest homeowners with a private, trained guard. Her host, Lord Windermere, and his younger brother Lord Avery Hill were among them, and both were extremely shrewd gentlemen. They would have the greatest influence on the others if Meriwether won their support this week.

As far as causes went, Meriwether was entitled to his opinion that such a service was needed. But the truly needy of London were most at risk from robbers and couldn't afford to pay for their own private guard. Truth to tell, she was finding it hard to support Meriwether's ambitions as completely as she once did. She'd also come to suspect their affair had become a way to gain entry into the upper ten thousand by association, a means to an end for him.

However disappointed she might feel about that and his motives, Esme would never allow herself to depend on a man for her entire happiness. If she wasn't involved with Meriwether, there was always someone handsome to fantasize about and encourage into her bed down the road. Over the years of her widowhood, she'd never lacked for male companionship.

She nodded to Lord Avery Hill and Miles Hammond as they strolled past. The glow of appreciation in both men's eyes practically shouted their interest and soothed away her hesitation to break with Meriwether. She'd easily find someone who wanted to be with *her*.

Lord Avery Hill moved toward Harriet and she smiled with understanding. The pair had been lovers on and off for years, and it seemed this year would be no different.

Mr. Miles Hammond, however, was another matter entirely. A friend of hers since the final days of her largely unhappy marriage, his inclusion in the house party guest list confounded her. He was not a particular favorite of their host, or even of his brother, yet all had seemed to be in quite a genial mood with each other since the party began. She'd have to find out why Hammond had been included.

She glanced about those gathered for tonight's ball. Champagne was being passed around freely and everyone seemed happy and infinitely agreeable to enjoy the party atmosphere to the fullest extent. Parties such as these were opportunities to mingle and conduct discreet liaisons without expectation of deeper, longer-term connections in many cases. It was all very civilized. As the quartet hired to play tonight tuned their instruments, she smiled. She might find her host a trifle wearying, but she could ignore the little irritations in Windermere's company, given her expectation of every other pleasure.

She moved away from the hall as new guests were welcomed by Oswin and turned her gaze on Windermere. Couldn't he see his nearest neighbors had arrived and needed to be introduced to the first-time guests?

But no, he remained watching Meriwether talk, a slight

frown on his face.

After a long moment, Lord Windermere cast a questioning glance her way, catching her watching him. Unwilling to be ruffled by his scrutiny, Esme stared back. Good God, those cornflower-blue eyes of his would render a lesser woman immobile if she was unprepared. Esme knew Windermere well though, well enough not to be affected by his handsome face. He knew he was attractive, too; he thought far too well of his appeal for her taste, and she sometimes stared at him overlong just to make him a tiny bit uncomfortable.

His grin faded slowly as she held his gaze and then his glance cut to those gathered about him and back to her, a question now in his eyes. Esme hid a smile, tipped her head in the direction of the hall, waiting for Windermere to catch on to why she stared at him so pointedly. It certainly wasn't for his looks alone.

He shook his head, as if clearing his mind of a thought, and hurried off to do his duty as host, leaving her laughing at his befuddlement.

The man needed a wife sooner rather than later to manage himself and his home affairs better. Someone to point him in the right direction from time to time, or even daily.

She turned back to her quarry only to be disappointed yet again. Meriwether was headed in the opposite direction. He snagged two glasses of champagne, glancing over his shoulder once or twice, as he navigated the crowd and slipped into the hall.

How sweet. Perhaps she'd misunderstood his preoccupation and he was arranging a private rendezvous for them both beyond the ballroom. Esme didn't require the fuss of a perfect seduction, but his hands on her body would be very fine tonight.

She moved toward him but again lost sight. Esme drew in a deep breath in frustration. It wasn't the first time the man had vanished so completely since they'd arrived two days ago.

The hallway beyond the drawing room was filled to bursting with chattering guests and she moved smoothly through them, nodding and speaking occasionally to some. While she admired the elegance and comforts to be found in Lord Windermere's home, she kept her eye out for Meriwether. She turned into the library, but the room was startlingly empty.

"Looking for me?" Windermere asked as he came to stand near. His gaze raked her from head to toe in the most gauche way.

Arrogant and presumptuous. "Hardly. You should pay more attention to your guests and the health of your servants."

Instead of taking the hint that she wasn't in the mood to talk, he caught her hand and raised it to his lips. His blue eyes danced with amusement. "I do love when you're friendly. How have you been, Esme?"

She scowled at him and withdrew her hand to her side. "I've not given you leave to use my first name and I am not of a mood to spar with you. Go back to your other guests for amusement and send your butler to his bed. Anyone can see he's on the verge of collapse tonight."

"I already banished Oswin to rest." He laughed suddenly. "Young Pip has assumed his duties until Collins comes up."

"Just as well," she replied, thankful for such sensible decisions at last.

"Only you would ever dare tell me what to do in my own home. I wanted to thank you for coming," Windermere murmured. "But to convince everyone we're not at odds, you will have to talk to me occasionally with a little less acid in your tone."

"We've spoken as much as needed to quell any gossip." She smiled at him. "Or was it your wish to have me chivvy you out of your mopes too."

"I will say again you were right." Windermere sighed and raked a hand through his dark, wavy hair. "You're enjoying rubbing my nose in that business with Lady Bartlett, aren't you?"

"Perhaps." She smothered a laugh. He hadn't wanted to believe he was being used until it was almost too late to extract himself from the connection. "You were so indignant that day, and after venting your pique at me, you charged down the street—on foot of all things, my man and your horse trailing after. I laughed for at least a whole day afterward. But I am sorry you were let down."

He inhaled sharply, his jaw clenching before he relaxed and shook his head. "No, you're not. You're positively gloating that you were proved right about her."

She allowed herself the briefest smirk. "You should learn to listen to good advice when you hear it, even if it comes from a direction you don't care for. I did try at first every subtle method I could imagine to make you really look at her figure and behavior. She wanted to trap you and almost did. An adventuress of her poor standard is not suitable to be your countess."

"I believe you wholeheartedly." He leaned closer, bracing one hand on the doorframe beside her head so she was partially trapped by his body. "In fact, I'm considering leaving the matter of who should be in that position in your capable hands."

She stared at him in shock. "You'd let me choose your wife for you?"

"Well, perhaps not a wife." He grinned and his attention dropped to her bust. "But I'm open to hearing your suggestion for my next lover. I seem to have the worst luck in that area and you seem to have developed an interest in those I take to my bed."

Esme laughed at his absurd suggestion and ignored the overwhelming urge to unbutton her gown for him. She did not lead a man on while involved with another, even if that *other* was leading her on a merry chase tonight. "You hardly need advice on that. Any pair of breasts will do. But next time, if the lady claims she's carrying your child, at least find out for sure she's speaking truthfully *before* you request a special license."

"Breasts come attached to the lady." He sighed again and drew back. "Given my near miss, I'm no longer confident I've the patience for marriage."

Last year, Esme had formed a suspicion about Lord Windermere, what set him to sigh so often when someone married or was heard to have fathered a son or daughter. He implied he lacked patience, but that probably wasn't true. There were countless other gentlemen of their acquaintance with both legitimate and illegitimate children attached to their names. Lord Windermere had not lived the life of a saint, but he had no children of his own that Esme had ever learned of.

She could sympathize with his situation, though she'd never let on or embarrass him by speaking of it. At his age, nearing three and forty years, he must have begun to worry for the succession, since his brother appeared even less ready to settle down than he was. After that, the estate and title fell to a cousin who hadn't the bearing of an earl, in her opinion, although he did possess a sweet wife and two sons already.

She didn't know what to say to make him feel better anyway because nothing really could. She'd long since accepted her own barren state as a certainty. "Things might be different with the right woman," she suggested gently. At least that is what well-meaning family had always advised her.

He shook his head then assumed the warm expression so common for him that lit up his eyes so brightly she wanted to draw closer. "So, are you going to tell me what you were looking for?"

She glanced away, glad he'd changed the subject and that

the uncomfortable personal conversation between them was over. She wouldn't confide in him about her exasperation with her lover, but Windermere had invited Meriwether knowing they were intimately involved. It should have been clear to him whom she'd be looking for. "I'll let you get back to tending your guests and charming your next dance partner."

He sighed dramatically. "You're a cruel woman but you are correct. I have obligations. Until we meet again."

Esme turned on her heel and left the library and Lord Windermere behind. If not for the lingering feeling of shared sadness, she didn't plan to think of him again tonight.

Chapter Two

Richard Hill, third Earl of Windermere, prowled his home, checking that everyone he'd invited to his house party ball was happy and felt welcome. The Gloucestershire estate was his pride and joy, and his annual summer event that had begun as just a few brief days with friends now stretched to a week or more, depending on the weather and the guests' willingness to be entertained.

He didn't mind other people enjoying the comforts of his home and his beds. He hoped to send each guest away in a better mood than when they'd first arrived. The season of balls and routes in London wearied a man, and at his age, he'd come to think of comfort first. Richard hosted his annual gathering as a means to foster deeper friendships in society and also to provide a respite from the pressures of life, so he never hurried anyone to be on their way and overlooked a great many indiscretions.

Bed hopping was a common practice among those who'd not married for love or had yet to find the one who centered their world. The anticipation of adventurous sex with no strings attached or expectations of marriage was an added bonus most of his guests took full advantage of. Richard had always indulged in the past, but this year he'd adjusted his expectations a little higher.

He needed a son more than a casual fling, but fatherhood was proving elusive, as was settling on a suitable bride to wed first. He would have almost blundered, if not for Esme. He'd thought Eleanor loved him, but she had lied to him about a babe—and everything else, he'd soon discovered.

He'd never felt more angry or humiliated as he had then.

Esme was his secondary goal for this year's party. He needed to make amends for the public spectacle he'd made of himself where she was concerned. Esme might often be a prickly, managing wench, whose opinion frequently differed from his own, but that was as far as any discord went between them. His outburst in Town over Eleanor's scheme had caused Lady Heathcote to lose support among the *ton*, and he was annoyed by the whispers of a broken affair between them. He'd not expected such a ridiculous assumption to be believed and spread about. By inviting Esme to the estate for the party, he intended to prove to one and all how ridiculous any falling out had been.

As he passed close to the front hall doorway, he was hailed by a familiar voice.

"Windermere, there you are, and a sight for sore eyes indeed in this mad crush."

Richard hurried forward and embraced his cousin, Mr. Adrian Hill. "I expected you both days ago," he told the man. "What kept you?"

When they drew apart, Hill's wife Carolyn stepped forward to kiss his cheek. "We spent a few days in Berkeley, taking in the sights, which made us a bit later than we'd hoped."

"It's lovely there, so I can understand the attraction to linger." He smiled. He'd only fleetingly wondered about their delay, and since he could see all was well with them, he wouldn't worry about them again. "I trust the servants are seeing your luggage is taken upstairs to your usual rooms."

"Collins assured us it would be done immediately."

Carolyn craned her neck to gawk at the guests. After a moment, her hand flew to her hair. "I must look a sight arriving in the middle of a ball wearing a carriage dress."

"You look lovely." Richard squeezed her arm then led them to the base of the stairs so they could retreat to their rooms and change for the ball. Unless… He turned to them. "I say, if you don't feel up to joining us for dancing tonight after the long day of travel, I completely understand. There is another smaller fete later this week too."

Carolyn smiled, her shoulders sagging. "You would not mind?"

Richard liked his cousin's wife very much so he nodded. She hated to let anyone down, but she always seemed fearful of disappointing him particularly. He'd no idea why. "I will catch up with you both tomorrow I am sure. Ask a footman to deliver a supper if you're hungry. There should be spirits aplenty in your room."

"Thank you, but we will both join the guests as soon as we have changed," Hill advised, straightened his shoulders as he glanced around the hall to see who was in attendance.

"Yes, of course, my dear," Carolyn quickly murmured, chin dropping.

Hill shook his hand and swiftly led his wife upstairs, an arm curled protectively about her back. Richard followed their progress with a heavy heart. They had actually met here under his roof and had been inseparable ever since their marriage. However, his cousin liked to do things his way, despite his wife's opposite feelings or rather obvious exhaustion.

Avery joined him and draped an arm about his shoulders. "No luck, still, in luring her away from Adrian's side," he whispered.

"Avery, do stop talking nonsense. She appears to be tired and I was merely concerned." He threw off Avery's embrace. "I'd never be interested in our cousin's wife and I strongly suggest, again, that you don't let anyone else think so either.

She's too devoted to Adrian to allow anything improper."

"She likes you, for some strange reason." His brother shrugged. "But the more the merrier has always been my motto."

"And doesn't every woman who accepts an invitation into your bed come to regret it later." Richard pursed his lips and glanced about to check who was nearby. "Stay away from her and find yourself a wife. A legal wife, rather than the family nonsense. You might just need an heir before too long."

Avery's eyebrows shot up. "It's you who needs the heir, not me."

"That there isn't one already should be a warning to us both." Why lie to his brother? It wasn't as if they hadn't discussed marriage and babies, the pressing need for them, before. He was getting a bit long in the tooth for having never sired a child.

Avery frowned at him. "Why do you resist the family traditions and go out to capture a bride?"

"The family traditions are perverse," he insisted, scowling at the idea. He drew close to his brother. "I will *not* abduct a woman, chain her to a tree stump, and fuck her while she hangs there helpless. That is not my idea of how to begin a *loving* marriage."

"Don't criticize what you haven't tried." Avery smirked. "I, however, will take full advantage of the excitement our family traditions inspire in the females of my acquaintance without the hindrance of a real marriage. You don't have to complete *all* that the ritual entails. What's a bit of dangling between friends, eh?"

"I won't do it." Richard stalked away, dissatisfaction gripping him. By tradition, the titleholder and heirs of the Windermere estate were to abduct, seduce and consummate their relationship in the forest on the east of the estate before they legally wed. In the dead of night, of all times. Richard had been sired in that manner, born four months after the wedding, as had his father and every earl before him for six generations. Even his cousin Adrian had taken his Carolyn to the wishing tree in pursuit of his heir. Nine months later, Carolyn was delivered of a son and Adrian had been smug ever since.

It was all nonsense, of course, that such a ritual would ensure the succession. Perpetuating the myth was something he'd never, ever subject a woman to. He wanted the practice to die with him.

He forced his disgust away and concentrated instead on being a good host. Occasionally, he saw Esme flitting about the crowd ahead of him, but for the most part she continued to keep a distance. She had not made it easy on him when he'd apologized. He'd been a fool, and a rude one, and she made no effort to hide her amusement.

Damn vexing wench. Always one step ahead of him no matter how hard he tried not to be trailing behind. She was a woman of passionate opinion and he never backed down without reason. Their frequent debates had gained notoriety for the *ton*, which was likely why society had assumed they were engaged in a heated affair that had turned sour as he'd stormed away from her London residence without his horse.

She'd been so right about his butler though. Oswin wasn't a young man anymore, and the late nights of the party and demanding guests were already taking a toll on his health. The man hinted he'd remain at his post until Richard had his heir, too, which was another worry. How much longer could it take to fall in love and make an heir the right way?

He found Esme in the crowd again. Despite the smile she bestowed on those around her, she seemed unhappy, and it surprised him that he noticed. She was usually bubbling over with energy when she was around the friends they shared.

He moved toward her, drawn in a way he wasn't used to. Meriwether was thankfully elsewhere, boring others with his tedious quest for a private guard in London. For the life of him, Richard could not work out why Esme was with the man. They must have next to nothing in common besides sex. "Ladies, I do hope you are having a pleasant evening."

Lady Heathcote promised she was but became distracted by another guest and turned away. He stared at her graceful back a moment, admiring the lovely curves before him and her pale-blonde hair fashioned into an elaborate style on the top of her head. She was the standard many young ladies should aspire too. She was never without a clever quip; never without her composure intact, no matter the circumstance.

That left him with Lady Ames for company. "Will you honor me with a dance tonight, Harriet?"

"At least you ask," she muttered under her breath before handing over the little cards his sister had passed out to all the ladies for tonight's event. Harriet's card was bare, not even Avery's name marked upon it, so he claimed the next set and a later one, and remained to converse with her until their dance was at last called.

Harriet had been coming to his estate for many years and while they were not particularly close, never once intimate, she had been his brother's longest romantic partner and he genuinely liked having her here. However, as they settled into the dance, he couldn't dismiss his partner's distraction. She sighed a great deal more than was required of the chore of dancing with him. He was concerned enough to ask about her current mood. "What's wrong?"

"Absolutely nothing, my lord," she responded quickly, a touch more bite to her words than called for. Harriet was not much like Esme, who ordinarily expressed every single disappointment she came across openly to him. She usually hid her feelings much better. "I'm having a lovely evening. Jillian has outdone herself on your behalf."

"She has and I'm very grateful," he murmured. "As you might imagine, Avery is no help at all."

Harriet dipped her face low, staring at his cravat as they danced, leaving Richard a clear view over her head. His brother stood on the sidelines chatting to Lady Small, a woman recently widowed and uninvolved. When they passed the pair by, Harriet sighed heavily. "I can believe it."

Was Avery's attention to the widow the cause of her low mood? If so, he wouldn't blame the woman for being put out. Avery should have asked Harriet to dance, since he'd been the one to invite her to the house party in the first place. "Avery's head is always turned by a pretty face, but it never stays there," he said, hoping to soothe Harriet's disappointment.

"But it turns so often it begs the question will he ever stop looking elsewhere first," Harriet replied in a voice edged with resignation.

"I don't know," he answered honestly. It was a pity Avery hadn't settled down with Harriet. The woman was good for him, but Avery wasn't exactly the most committed man to any woman. He and Avery were poles apart in nature and attitude on that score. Avery was wild. Richard had responsibilities he couldn't shirk much longer. He needed an heir.

He changed the subject. "Have you everything you need in your room?"

"Yes, the room is as comfortable as ever. Thank you. I've always enjoyed coming to Windermere each year." She frowned. "But I have not seen Mr. and Mrs. Adrian Hill as yet. Are they visiting too this year?"

"They arrived not half an hour ago. They stopped on the journey in Berkeley, and Carolyn appears quite done in. I suggested they skip the party but Adrian assured me they would join us soon."

"She's a woman with child, or was when she last wrote to me, so the journey would have tired her," Harriet murmured, her gaze drawn across the floor to where Avery now danced enthusiastically with a red-faced Lady Small.

She stared then shook her head. "Would you excuse me, and from our next dance too? I urgently need to speak with Carolyn."

"Yes, of course I don't mind. By all means, seek them out." Richard escorted Harriet from the floor before the dance ended and followed her progress as she weaved through the crowd and swiftly disappeared.

While he rejoiced at the news his cousin's wife would have a third child, he was also swept up in a wave of sadness. No wonder Hill had supported his wife on the stairs. He was looking out for his growing family.

The one that will replace mine and take the title from us if we don't father our offspring first.

Richard swallowed his bitter pill of resignation and went in search of a worthy distraction to dull the ache of wanting a son to follow after him.

Maybe he should try the wishing tree at least once, just to be sure lack of faith, for want of a better term, wasn't the only problem with him.

Chapter Three

———◆———

Esme searched the remaining public rooms for Meriwether, but she found no sign of him. Disappointed and more than a bit put out from the fruitless chase, she retraced her steps to the ballroom and mingled with the crowd while admiring the dancers twirling beneath Windermere's triple chandeliers.

Although asked more than once to take a turn upon the floor, she declined the invitations. She wasn't in the mood for that kind of dancing. She'd much rather do something more intimate and invigorating and in private with her lover.

She huffed out a breath. *If he could be persuaded to stay by my side long enough.*

Her favorite footman in Lord Windermere's employ, a young brother to her indispensible Penny, appeared and presented her with a glass of blessedly cold champagne.

"Thank you, Pip," she murmured as she gratefully sipped her drink. "Did you manage to spend any time with your sister yet?"

"Not much, my lady," he whispered back.

The preparations for tonight's ball generally involved all the staff and allowed little time for any servant to stand around idly chatting, even to a member of their own family. Pip and Penny Bradshaw were all the family they had, and they'd been apart a year. "Tomorrow will be easier for Penny. I will sleep late so you'll have ample time to catch up in the morning."

"You're very generous, my lady."

She winked. "Anything to prevent your sister sighing so loudly when she misses you when we leave again. Anyone would think you'd gone off to war instead of gaining a position in a beautiful country estate like this."

He smothered a laugh, for he knew his sister's habit of wild exaggeration all too well, and then turned away to continue serving the guests champagne.

Esme was very proud of how the young man had turned out. Pip had spent a few months in her home under the tutelage of her senior staff, acquiring the polish to gain himself a better position than she could offer. He'd been successful in winning over Windermere's staff and gained employment as a footman, but she knew his ambition was for a butler's position to make his sister proud.

Esme made her way to Lady Small's side, where she stood alone, clapping along as a dance ended. "Quite the gathering, isn't it, my dear? Did you by chance notice where Harriet went? I have not seen her for a while."

Lady Small's expression was one of sour disapproval. "I expect she is entertaining Lord Avery Hill in his bedchamber by now."

More than likely. "You disapprove?"

"Indeed I do." Lady Small shivered. "Do you know what that man dared suggest to me? I'm in utter shock still."

Lord Avery Hill had a penchant for speaking bluntly of his sexual adventures and appetite. Some women liked that sort of thing, others not so much. "That often happens when one speaks to him for the first time," Esme informed her in all seriousness. "Consider it a test of character. I'm sure he will not be so brazen again."

"It's scandalous," Lady Small hissed. "And to suggest a dalliance with someone else in the room too."

Ah, he'd suggested a ménage a trois. "Each to their own." Esme shrugged. "Don't make up your mind that you won't like something until you've at least tried it once."

Lady Small stared at her in shock. "I don't think so."

"You might be pleasantly surprised by the experience," she murmured. Esme had tried, but preferred to be the center of attention for one man only.

The crowd quieted suddenly and she looked about them in surprise. The quartet that had been playing in competition with the crowd's noise trilled a few notes and fell silent too. All the guests faced the far side of the room, and since a broad, masculine back blocked her view, Esme stepped up beside the man, noticing belatedly that Lord Windermere had been close enough to likely eavesdrop on her conversation with Lady Small.

A hearty male voice called for attention and Esme stretched to see who dared interrupt the dancing. Sir Jeffrey Follows, a local knight who'd joined them for several dinners in past years, kept clearing his throat rather importantly. "If I could have your attention please," he said at last. "It gives me great pleasure to announce that Mr. Albert Meriwether has asked for my daughter, Jane's, hand in marriage, and I have given them my blessing. He shall marry our darling girl before the month is out."

Esme froze as everyone else clapped, unable to believe what she'd heard. Meriwether smiled at Jane with a satisfied expression on his face.

The heartless scoundrel. How could he stand there as his marriage was announced without warning her first?

"I guess he wasn't yours after all," Lady Small whispered in her ear cruelly.

Esme fumed. How could he embarrass her in such a way? He had never hinted he was involved with any other lady and certainly never mentioned a wish to marry. If he had, she'd never have slept with him. By morning she would be the laughingstock of the entire house party.

Windermere held out his arm. "A good match," he mused aloud. "Come, my dear Esme. Shall we toast the happy match in private?"

Although surprised by Windermere's support at such a moment, she was grateful for the lifeline he offered. She needed to get out of the room before she said or did something she'd regret. She could not wish Meriwether happiness. Not in her current temper. She needed a good excuse to slip away and give vent to her irritation in private.

She placed her arm through Lord Windermere's and allowed him to lead her from the room, satisfied beyond reason when they passed Lady Small. The woman stood with her mouth agape.

When they reached the entrance hall, he squeezed her hand and glanced around. "Almost out of earshot. Just a bit farther. Did I show you the new paintings in my bedchamber?"

His question cut straight through her anger. She raised her eyes to his. "I've never visited your bedchamber before, Windermere, and you know it."

He grinned. "Then you must come. Multiple times, I think."

She drew away from him. "Don't imagine—"

His expression turned serious and he chivvied her up the staircase. "It's the fastest way to cut off spiteful gossip. If we are both noticeably absent for a while, there's something else for my guests to talk about. Deprive them of their fun at your expense with a different tale of conquest."

"You knew about him?"

He took her arm and sped her up the next flight of stairs. "Not about the marriage. That caught me by surprise, and I would have spoken of it if I'd had any inkling. I must say I am not unhappy about it. The damned fool was hardly deserving of your intimate company."

She reached the next landing before her head cleared enough to consider the right reply. "And you believe you deserve me?"

"Oh, no." He laughed and released her. "I fully expect you to toss me over as early as tomorrow. I'll make a long face while you can claim my arrogance off-putting or something harmless. A few well-told exaggerations and all will be well."

Esme glanced around to confirm they were alone. "Why would you do this for me?"

He sighed and set his hands behind his back while leaning forward a little to look her in the eye. "Because I remember that you once tried to prevent me from looking foolish, and I appreciate that."

"You are not making sense, sir."

He drew close to her ear, his breath hot against her skin. "Wouldn't you rather have your revenge on Meriwether without risk? Would an affair with me tweak his nose?"

What Windermere suggested had merits, and if there was no risk involved…

He smiled wickedly as he drew back. "It is clear you expected the house party to proceed in the normal fashion. I thought Meriwether understood your rules. You rather famously don't dally with married men, or engaged-to-be-married men, so his assumption shows a distinct misunderstanding of your character. He should have warned you of the impending wedding announcement and didn't. That makes him not particularly admirable in my book. Come with me, let other's believe we've patched up our differences in bed. I cannot believe I invited him."

"Why *did* you invite him?"

"To make *you* happy, I thought." He tilted his head to the side. "Now, instead, I think we shall have fun at his expense."

"You seem to have a knack for revenge."

He winked. "It is a spur-of-the-moment feeling,

encouraged by your long face. We would not have to actually be intimate. Only my guests need to be convinced we are."

Esme forced a smile to her face, but it was a brittle thing. Windermere's plan would help her save face, and if he did not expect intimacies then their relationship would remain the same. For a change, the man made sense. "Where might your chambers be located?"

"I thought you'd never ask." He linked their arms, drawing her closer to his side, a wicked smile playing across his lips. "This way. I claimed this part of the east wing after the redecoration last year. My brother and sister claimed everything else."

That was a lot of manor house to have given up. "Surely not."

He opened a door to her with a short bow. "Well, perhaps I exaggerate just a touch. A man must be allowed some idiosyncrasies."

"You have more than a few." Esme stepped into his apartment and gasped at the Spartan interior. She had heard some people enjoyed uncluttered spaces, but Windermere's sitting room was bare and his bedchamber, when she reached it, held only a bed. There were no looking glasses to be found on the walls. No small furniture of any kind. Just one huge bed and a blazing fire that sent flickering light to all corners of the room.

She turned to regard Lord Windermere curiously. She'd never imagined him a frugal man.

His smile was a touch uncertain. "I prowl about in my sleep and crash into things."

Esme frowned. Now *that* she hadn't heard about him. "Really?"

"Unfortunately, yes. I'd offer you a chair if I had one, but won't you make yourself at home?" He indicated the bed was where she should sit and with no other options available, Esme perched on the edge. Windermere loosened his cravat. "I feel compelled to apologize. I had no idea about Jane and Meriwether, though he was much in her company yesterday, come to think of it. Jane is sweet enough in her own way, but I'm rather annoyed that they announced the marriage without a word of warning or even asking my permission. I've no interest in turning my house party ball into their engagement celebration. I find that extremely presumptuous."

Esme let her dancing slippers fall from her feet and then comfortably tucked her legs beneath her. She stripped off her gloves for good measure and flexed her fingers. "Yes, I can see they were extremely discourteous to you."

He came closer. "And to you. Are you very much upset?"

The fact that she had to consider her answer before she spoke proved her heart had survived the disappointment. "My pride perhaps."

He sighed and leaned against the bed. "Good. I—"

A discreet panel in the painted wall opened and the butler hurried in, arms full of firewood. He froze when he discovered his master wasn't alone. "Forgive me, my lord. I had no idea you'd retired for the night."

Windermere scowled. "Oswin, do get out. I sent you to bed, not to replace my valet."

The butler cast a curious glance at Esme before he all but ran from his master's presence.

Windermere pursed his lips momentarily and then laughed. "There. Any suggestion you were disappointed by Meriwether will vanish for good. By morning the talk of the house party will be of a certain fetching lady who was seen gracing my bed. Isn't that easy?"

Esme leaped from the bed. "Then I shall see you tomorrow."

He caught her arm. "To be convincing, you'd have to stay a bit longer. I do have a reputation as an eager lover to protect, too."

She stilled. He did have a point, and Lord Windermere

should not come out of this arrangement with his reputation besmirched yet again. They would both benefit if she stayed a little longer. "That is true."

His grip loosened and he teased the inside of her arm with a soft caress, setting gooseflesh sweeping over her skin.

Eventually his hand fell away, his expression growing speculative. Esme was almost certain he hadn't wanted to release her. Yet, becoming intimately involved with Lord Windermere was a ridiculous idea. She did appreciate his help tonight, but there was a limit to what she'd do for revenge. And if they were intimate, Windermere would be unbearably smug afterward.

She climbed back onto the bed and raised her hands to her hair to remove a pin that had grown uncomfortable. After further consideration, she removed all of them to let her hair tumble down her back and shook out her blonde locks. "Emerging from your bedchamber in a completely disheveled state, and needing my maid to set me to rights again, would be better than appearing barely ruffled too. If we are to perpetuate a lie, the rumors of our time together as lovers might as well be exceptional. Tell me about the paintings."

"My sister is the artist." Windermere held out a hand and, bemused, she dropped the pins into his palm. He strolled toward the mantle and placed them there, then shrugged out of his evening jacket. "As you can see, she's recently found a way to decorate without giving me movable objects to damage, and simply paints on the walls."

"This must have taken some time." Esme admired the extraordinary work around them. "Your sister is very clever."

"Don't tell her," he warned with a laugh, dropping his jacket to the floor in a careless heap. "She'll want to paint the rest of the estate the same way and I like being the recipient of unique gifts."

Esme fell back on the mattress and wriggled, ensuring her gown would be suitably rumpled at the back. If this were her bedchamber, she'd have Jillian paint lovely clouds on the ceiling with a cherub or two peeking from behind each one. "Of course you do. Always thinking of yourself first and foremost."

"Not always," Windermere murmured in a low, deep voice that sent alarming sensations racing over her skin. The next moment, he flung himself on the bed at her side. "The project kept her busy during her mourning, but I don't want her to spend her life here, hiding from being hurt again."

She turned her face to his. "She'll embrace her life when she's ready."

His blue eyes softened. "Is that what you did when Heathcote passed?"

She grimaced and looked up again. "Heathcote and I were strangers long before then, so I…went through the motions for the sake of appearances."

"I had a feeling you'd say that," Windermere murmured, capturing her hand and squeezing. "He wasn't a warm man, was he?"

"To his mistress he was." She winced again. Sometimes the pain of her husband's betrayal caught her by surprise, as it did now. "I prefer not to think about him if you don't mind."

"Of course," he murmured, then filled the next hour with harmless chatter about the party, their mutual acquaintances, and the entertainments organized for the coming days.

Everything but the fact they were still holding hands.

Chapter Four

———◆———

Richard braced his hands on the stone bannister above the great ballroom and scanned the exuberant crowd twirling below. He had made sure he'd invited an equal numbers of ladies and gents for the ten-day house party. But to his chagrin, the ladies he'd considered his best chances for improving his acquaintance with had already paired off with other men while he'd been locked away with Esme, pretending to enjoy a jolly romp in his bed.

Damn Esme and her long face.

He hadn't thought through his decision to save Esme from embarrassment properly and paid the price for it now. Although he had to admit that the chaste encounter hadn't been entirely a waste of time. He thought, perhaps, he and Esme had reached an accord over the past. He felt entirely better for that and looked forward to more civil conversation with the lady in the future.

"I think the party is a resounding success," Jillian, his younger sister, murmured as she looked over the assembled guests with pride shining on her face.

A great deal of the arrangements for the party had fallen into her capable hands and he was pleased to see her in such good spirits. She'd been entirely too quiet since returning home following the death of her husband of three years. Benjamin's death last winter had knocked the joy from her eyes and he could almost see it glimmering there again. "You've exceeded my expectations, little sister. Very well done indeed."

He saw nothing but disappointment below him though. The woman he'd invited with the secret purpose of considering for marriage, Lady Beatrice Small, was dancing in the arms of someone else, and, given what he'd heard of her unguarded opinions to Esme earlier in the evening, Richard had concluded Beatrice be a great deal too much trouble as a wife.

He couldn't marry a prudish woman. Oh, no indeed. He needed a sensible, open-minded woman who was not easily offended. His brother Avery was bound to frighten away any timid souls he might consider for his wife, so he had to choose with his head too. "I think this might be our last year. What do you say to a summer by the sea next year?"

Jillian, unaware of the source of his disappointment, laughed outright at his suggestion. "You love showing off the estate, and summer wouldn't be the same without this event and our friends visiting."

As he glanced down, he spotted the prickly, if occasionally lovely Esme, speaking with the friends she'd made among the locals over the past years of visits. His cousins had finally made an appearance and the pair hung on her every word. She charmed everyone she met, made them feel like wanted, desirable companions—all except him, normally.

A pity, that. He *had* owed Esme the favor of rescue from embarrassment.

Esme had saved him from a grievous mistake. He still felt the fool for being nearly duped into marrying a woman who pretended to be carrying his child.

He was still astonished Esme had thought him worth rescuing in the first place.

Damn Esme for revealing her hurt feelings.

His sister nudged his arm. "Don't skulk about like this. Go and mingle with your guests."

"Soon," he murmured, distracted by Esme's warm smile to Mr. Miles Hammond, who'd joined her little group. He tensed at the ease between them. Esme and Hammond were very old friends and frequent companions around London of late. He was fairly sure they'd never been lovers, but with Esme one could never be certain of anything. Until tonight's farce with him, she'd always been incredibly discreet in her affairs. "Tell me why I invited Hammond again?"

"Because he is Esme's friend and you thought having him here, too, would lend her support," Jillian said with a laugh. "He's actually very nice once you can get him to talk."

As if sensing his scrutiny, Hammond glanced up to where they stood. He stared a moment and then nodded before returning to hang on Esme's conversation.

Richard's tension remained. *That man.* Richard could never decide whether to like Hammond or not.

When Jillian was drawn away by Lord Hogan to dance, Richard watched her go with a wry chuckle. His sister had a suitor chasing after her. Lord Hogan had been keeping a rather close proximity to her these past months since she'd packed away her black gowns and started to embrace life again. Always at her elbow, always interested in what she was doing. Richard wouldn't mind the connection, should the man propose, which was why he'd also been invited for the week, to see what might come of the connection.

He tapped his fingers along the balustrade as he made his way to the dance floor below. He did not want to spend the night watching lovers flirt and sneak away to quiet corners. If he could not have a wife, he wanted to lose himself in the arms of someone who did not expect a commitment from him.

Or, if that were not possible, he'd rather spend the night with someone who challenged his mind. That meant his best chance of amusement tonight was sparring with Lady Heathcote.

Damn Esme for being so damn intriguing.

He'd always fought the attraction, but tonight he was feeling distinctly adventurous. Since their interlude on his bed, he'd wanted to get under her skin in the worst way, and not just to earn another scowl.

Once he reached the ballroom floor, he scanned the crowd. Esme had moved on from his cousins and was currently out of sight. Irritating woman. Why could she never be where he expected her to be? She was like every other woman he'd known. Always making him chase after them for a bit of attention.

It comforted him that she wasn't with Hammond, who was leading some other lady to the dance floor.

Without the hope of even uncivil conversation, Richard stepped out onto the terrace to enjoy the moonlight alone.

Or so he first thought.

Ahead along the terrace, Esme stood just outside the ballroom windows, looking in through a distant set. Candlelight played over her face and he could tell by the way her head tilted that her attention followed the dancers inside. She did not turn to greet him as Richard approached her. He stopped close behind and shared her view.

Meriwether and his intended bride pranced on his dance floor, looking as smitten as young lovers were supposed to do. His cousin's strolled past, arm in arm, with only eyes for each other.

"The party is going well," she murmured without turning or taking her eyes from the dancers.

Jillian and Lord Hogan danced past next. "So it seems."

"Warn your sister away from Hogan if you can." She sighed. "He will not be good for her."

He bristled. Although he should have listened to Esme about his last lover, there was only so much advice a bachelor could stand, particularly when it concerned members of his own family. "They're just dancing."

"That's how it starts." Esme shook her head. "He's all wrong for her, but she likely won't know it until it's too late." Meriwether and his future bride twirled past and she shook her head again. "Or she will, and won't act on her intuition to run."

When Esme still did not turn away, Richard caught her hand and tugged. Staring after the one you lost only led to one's friends considering you a fool. Esme was hardly that, but in case her heart had truly been involved with Meriwether, and wounded, Richard would be the one to do the saving this time.

If she allowed him.

"Come away," he whispered.

Her lashes lowered over her eyes and her grip on his fingers tightened.

He tugged again and thankfully she followed him toward the terrace stairs and out into the moonlit gardens without raising a fuss. *A remarkable feat.*

Richard led her away from the house, strolling through the still gardens with little thought to direction. It was blessedly peaceful after the chaos of the ball and he was glad to share a few more rare quiet moments with Esme.

Eventually they came upon the river house, clinging to the edge of the fast-moving stream, where they could talk and be comfortable. He led her to the steps.

She peered at the building then lifted her face to his. "My, my. This is intriguing."

The timber building had once been used by boatmen on a daily basis, but had fallen into disuse long ago. Richard liked to come here to think, and especially so since his recent near brush with matrimony. He'd spent quite a lot of time in the river house and never gave the dark interior too much thought. He'd had several creature comforts installed. Esme would not find the interior too rustic. "Are you afraid to be alone with me again?"

"Hardly."

Richard grinned. Esme was quite the adventurer and she'd never minced words. She also didn't seem to care where they were going. This was so much better than watching couples dance and sneak away for pleasure. Perhaps he and Esme could work up the energy to have a rousing good discussion by the end of the night. He could be satisfied at least with that and looked forward to a stirringly good one.

He unlatched the door and, still holding her arm tightly, led her up the shallow steps. Inside was black as pitch. He took her with him to the shuttered river-front windows and threw them wide. Moonlight and stars gleamed, lightening the shadowed space into something remarkable. He'd thought this place fascinating as a boy, even more so with a pretty woman on his arm.

His breath caught as he stared down at Esme. Without the scowl, she really was a very beautiful woman. "What do you think?"

Esme paced the chamber, returning to the window to stare out at the fast-moving water sliding past. "Breathtaking. It's as if no one else exists." She leaned as far out as she could and sighed.

Fearing *how* far she might lean, and knowing what dangers awaited her immediately below the window, he caught her by the back of her gown and held on tightly. "Be careful."

She settled back on her heels. "I assume the current is too fast to make swimming pleasant."

"The rain last week has made that inadvisable for the party but during a dry stretch, it is not so bad a little farther downstream." He smoothed her gown over her back where he'd gripped her, then spread his hands over her shoulders. She was quite soft, something that hadn't sprung to mind when they'd argued. He was also startled to feel the beginnings of desire.

For Esme?

Would surprises never cease tonight?

He teased her delicate skin with his thumb and was rewarded with a shudder. Richard had never spent much time alone in Esme's company and as his cock thickened with arousal, he wondered why. His attraction to her tonight took him by surprise. Tension always built swiftly between them, but this was not the usual prelude to hostilities. The idea of arguing with Esme had been replaced by a much better one.

Anticipation licked along his skin. He inhaled the scent of rosewater that clung to her hair. "Jillian used to swim with us when she was much younger, but prefers to laugh at us when we complain of the cold afterward."

"I quite agree with her thinking," Esme murmured. "I don't much care for the cold myself."

Richard eased closer a half-step. Esme leaned back into his chest. Cautiously, he slid one arm around her waist. The anticipation of holding her even closer yet caught firmly in his mind. From all he'd heard, all he'd seen of her character, Esme would not play games other than those of the erotic variety. For an affair, Esme would be a wise choice, and she was suddenly without a lover now that Meriwether was promised elsewhere.

He brought his free hand to her neck and stroked the backs of his fingers over her throat.

"Windermere," Esme whispered in an annoyed tone. "What do you think you're doing?"

"I think I'd like to make love to you, if you don't mind."

"I don't think that's wise," she warned, but didn't pull away.

"Don't make up your mind that you won't like something until you've at least tried it once." He laughed softly. "Isn't that what you told Lady Small to do earlier in the night?"

"Listening in?" she complained.

"I agree wholeheartedly." He'd never so much as kissed

Esme before and he was desperate to taste her suddenly. Richard bowed his head slowly and set his lips to her neck. He nibbled her skin as she shuddered. "You don't have to say anything. Just let it happen."

Chapter Five

Just let it happen. If all of Esme's liaisons began this easily, she'd never have reason to be discontent.

Lord Windermere's breath teased her skin and tempted her to set aside all the reasons why an affair with him wasn't wise. She did not wish to become another conquest for the earl, but she was still peevish and in need of an outlet for her frustration. Sex had always been her preferred method to rid herself of irritation, and he had offered nicely.

His suggestion too had loosened something reckless inside her that she'd never known existed. A desire to break her own rules grew. To experience something new without forethought or planning had never been her way. But Windermere's offer did tempt her. She knew him very well. She was aware of his character, his failings and values. Society at large assumed they'd been intimate, but they each knew there had never been any intention of that.

Until now.

He curled his fingers about her waist in a soft caress that left her wanting more. She closed her eyes as he did it again with more conviction.

A shock of want consumed her. She wanted his hands on her skin, his body entwined with hers, the thrill of fulfilled desire soon to follow. Esme had never considered Windermere as a potential lover. An annoyance, certainly. A man with whom to spar when she felt peevish, as she did now; not that she'd ever admit that as the sole reason she'd enjoyed finding fault with him in the past. Yet tonight she was hard-pressed to find a reason to deny him because she wasn't satisfied yet. He'd been kind and his timing and understanding of her mood had been excellent. Who would have thought he might interpret her needs so well?

Sharing a bed would change things between them.

She would know his taste, the sound of his pleasure. The most intimate of knowledge only possible when a man and a woman had lain together and driven each other wild.

She turned in his arms. An expectant grin twisted his lips, making him appear boyish and even more attractive. Her pulse raced with anticipation as she saw the gleam of hope in his eyes. "This would mean nothing."

"Of course." He swooped to kiss her, their first ever, and the initial brush of his lips turned every angry feeling to flames of a far more worthy emotion.

Desire. A hot, living flame consumed her. She kissed him back, holding his head to hers so he couldn't get away. He stroked his tongue into her mouth, tasting her, and she did the same to him. Esme threaded her fingers through his dark, wavy hair and clenched the locks tightly.

Windermere pressed her against the window frame at her back. His hands framed her face, his thumbs caressing her cheeks as he drove his tongue into her mouth again and again. He drew back and one thumb slipped to the corner of her lips. Esme turned her head and took it into her mouth, sucking hard on his flesh until he moaned.

It had been a long time, perhaps forever, since Esme had ever wanted a man so desperately or so immediately as she did now.

Windermere cupped her breasts and warmth pooled between her legs when he squeezed them with firm pressure. She pulled him back to kiss and boldly stroked her tongue into his mouth to taste him once more. He squeezed her nipple through the gown and that excited her enough to release what was left of her hesitation and chase after what was being offered so boldly.

She stripped off her gloves so she could really feel him.

A ragged groan left Windermere's throat as she allowed his tongue to invade her again and then she mimicked fucking him with her mouth. He clutched her body to his, holding her head firmly. His aggression and need gave her the thrill of holding power over him. Some men treated her too gently. He did not seem that way. Esme liked a man who was committed to her pleasure in bed, and straightforward about what he wanted in return.

He hoisted her into his arms, leaving her feet barely touching the ground. When he grasped her backside and pressed her against him, she discovered him aroused. Being wanted this desperately was exactly what Esme needed. Lust was always a balm for a wounded pride and she had been feeling sorely disappointed lately. When he lifted his head from the kiss, he was grinning, his eyes alight with mischief.

He propelled them into the shadows and when her legs bumped against something hard and heavy enough not to move, Windermere eased his grip to one of eager exploration. His next kiss gave her no time to reconsider but, given his enthusiasm, she hardly wanted to. He thumbed her nipples, kneaded her breasts as if they were ripe fruit.

She twined her arms about his neck and gave herself up to his desire and control. A little passion couldn't possibly change things between them in any meaningful way. They'd both had many lovers. She could still find fault with him later and by tomorrow evening, either one of them might have moved on to someone else. She expected nothing more than a little passion from him tonight. There was no reason to expect more.

With one hand cupping her head and the other sliding firmly down her back, Windermere set her body aflame. He drew her against the hard swell of his erection, and ground her against his length.

Windermere pinched her nipple hard through her gown and she gasped in shock and delight. She tightened her grip on his thick hair and made love to his mouth with the intention of never stopping, no matter what he did to the rest of her body.

He broke the kiss suddenly, turned her around, and pressed close against her back. "Can't think when you do that."

His hands slid everywhere: over the fabric of her gown to cup her breasts, low to tease her sex with a possessive touch. He bent and caught her skirts, dragging the fabric up her legs with a thick, desperate groan. The warmth of his palms on her inner thighs made her body quake and a ragged gasp escaped her control. He boldly teased her curls, slid his fingers between her lower lips and demanded immediate entry. Esme closed her eyes, astonished by how delightful she found his technique and how willing she was for him. She was filled with impatience, her body restless and hot.

"Esme," he whispered hoarsely against her neck then nipped her skin. "Touch me."

She knew what he wanted without having to ask where. Despite the awkwardness of the task, Esme put her hands behind her back, grasped the fastenings of his trousers to release his cock from confinement. She caught his length in one hand, pumping his flesh languidly, and discovered he needed little encouragement to moan. He was thick, hard and long, quite possibly perfectly proportioned though she'd never dare mention that to him.

Windermere fought to bring them closer, shoving her gown up to her waist so they were skin to skin, her flesh pressed to the burning heat of his. He lifted one of her feet to a chair, opening her body. As he pressed his cock inside her, a flicker of astonishment filled Esme at his haste. She ordinarily did not like to rush penetration with a new lover. It was over too quickly, often lacking the passion she craved and a degree of closeness she found necessary to find release.

His initial thrusts were deep and fast but soon slowed. Sliding out until almost leaving her body then back in as deeply as it was possible to be connected to her. He took his time, drawing out their passion so well that Esme was in heaven. She had little to do but accept and encourage. His fingers remained on her clitoris, teasing on and off so she was never too close to the brink of release. She wrapped her hand around his thigh where it pressed hard against hers and kept him close.

Esme curled one arm over her head and tangled her fingers in his hair again. He might be in danger of marking her skin with his kisses and little nips but that only added to her excitement. The chair teetered forward from the force of his movements, so far that Esme feared they'd topple over entirely before he finished with her.

But Windermere never allowed her to fall. He held her so tightly that they barely parted a moment for each thrust. The discovery of his hunger only made her crave his touch more.

She tugged hard on his hair.

Her reward was a deep, dark masculine growl. "Woman, you're driving me wild."

Their thighs slapped together loudly as his thrusts quickened. Esme braced herself on the chair, little caring that she was crying out or that Windermere was grunting too. This was exactly what she'd needed—a man to make her forget everything else.

"Come for me," he demanded as he stilled inside her. "I will wait for you and then withdraw."

Chills raced over her body at his words. He would withdraw to spare her an unwanted pregnancy, but such an action, one that would curtail his pleasure, wasn't necessary.

She had been with many men and, although some withdrew for the same reason Windermere gave, she had never conceived before. "I am barren, Windermere. There's no danger of a child."

Windermere tightened his grip around her hips. He didn't speak, just held her close as if uncertain whether to believe her or not.

Esme had had a long time to accept her situation. She didn't need his doubt or his pity, she needed his passion more.

She slipped her fingers beneath his where they'd stilled on her sex and she stoked her clitoris herself. His fingers joined hers soon after, teasing in tandem. Windermere's hot breath blistered her nape. The sensation of being utterly surrounded by him sped her release. When he rolled his hips, her body clenched around his cock and she thrashed in his arms. As her desire peaked, she shrieked his name, something she rarely did with a lover.

He began thrusting as soon as she quieted. His lips slid away from her neck as he groaned heavily against the top of her spine and spilled his seed deep inside her. He held her tightly against him as he dragged in deep, gasping breaths.

"Dear God," he whispered hoarsely. "Imagine what we might feel with the comforts of a proper bed around us."

Content to be held a while, Esme stroked the arm wrapped around her waist and then began to laugh. She'd had no idea his reputation was so well-deserved when it came to desire. Not even the revelation of her barren state had truly distracted him from his passion.

For herself, truth be told, she was feeling a little unbalanced by their romp and her confession. She usually didn't mention she couldn't have children in the heat of the moment. It tended to throw cold water over most men's amorous moods. "I think once was enough, don't you?"

He softly kissed her cheek before he disengaged and righted his clothing. When he drew close again after she'd straightened herself, he whispered, "I don't think I could say no to you if I ever had the chance again. Think of me tonight and let me know tomorrow?"

She met his gaze. The man stared at her, his blue eyes compelling her to agree with him. Esme's opinion of him wavered a little in his favor. "Perhaps."

Chapter Six

"**P**lease, don't be vulgar." Esme adjusted the collar of her Spencer and admired her reflection carefully in the early morning light. For a woman her age, nearing six and thirty, she was relieved to see her late-night cavorting with Lord Windermere had no visible effect on her outward appearance.

"I thought we agreed to share all our secrets," Harriet protested. "I cannot ignore that you dallied with our host, a singularly mind-boggling decision on your part. I thought you didn't particularly care for him, and certainly not in that way."

Esme faced the mirror, picked up a firm-bristled brush and stroked it over each eyebrow carefully, forcing the fine hairs straight. Her blue eyes were bright with the energy welling beneath her skin. "He *is* arrogant."

"Well, I imagine he'll be far worse now that he's had you." Harriet slumped back in her chair with a huff. "They all are. Whatever possessed you to become intimate with a Hill?"

He'd asked nicely? No, she couldn't admit to that out loud. Harriet would fall all over herself with laughter and make fun of her for months to come. She was aware of how often she'd criticized her current host in the privacy of their respective bedchambers. It was too often to pass unnoticed that she wasn't feeling particularly indifferent toward him today.

She felt excited, as if she stood on a precipice and whatever lay below was a mystery. She scoffed. There was no mystery surrounding Windermere. She was intimately acquainted with every aspect of his personal life. His taste, the feel of his hands on her hips, the rasping desperation of his voice as he commanded her during intimacy, sent a thrill of desire through her body even now.

Her pussy tingled with anticipation yet again. At least the tenth time since awakening alone that morning. A singular romp shouldn't have overset her sense this much. Later she would think about the encounter properly, with a rational mind and cooler logic to place the event where it belonged—a memorable encounter and nothing more serious. When Harriet wasn't around to pick apart her feelings about Windermere, she might make sense of them and him.

She was *not* friends with Windermere, nor ever likely to be. The unlikeliest of lovers. Even so...

"He caught me at a weak moment." Esme frowned at her friend. "What are you doing up and about before midday? I didn't expect to see you recovered from last night's revels for a few more hours yet."

Harriet's smile slipped away. "I couldn't sleep."

Esme turned back to her mirror and secured a gold pendant around her neck. "Has Avery been that wicked again? There are laws against some of the things he likes, you know."

"That wouldn't stop him," Harriet said quietly. "Esme, I have broken with him completely. I told him I'd never share his bed again."

"What?" She spun about. "When?"

Harriet wrung her hands. "Last night, actually. I

couldn't find you. I suppose you must have been in Windermere's arms by then."

Esme immediately shifted to sit at her side and threw an arm around her shoulders. Harriet and Lord Avery Hill had been intermittent lovers for a long time. Such a change was unexpected. "But why? Did he do something wrong? Did he hurt you?"

The other woman shrugged then she looked away. "Not the way you imagine."

Esme caught her chin and turned her face back to hers. "Who did he invite to join you both last night? You know I'll not tell a soul."

"It is not who he invites, it is that he always does. We want very different things from life." She shuddered. "Esme, do you ever worry that the reason we are both still alone is because we're too particular?"

"Is that what he suggested you were?" Esme shook her head in disgust. "I doubt Lord Avery Hill could have found a more open-minded bed partner anywhere. I certainly wouldn't put up with his wandering eye the way you have, or his penchant for indulging in romps with more than one partner at a time."

"I won't ever be enough for him."

Esme caught her hand and squeezed it. "And he has never appreciated what he had in you."

"That is what I realized last night. I had a painful decision to make, and in the end he made it easy for me to give him up for something better." Her smile grew brittle. "But in light of my choice, it might be uncomfortable for me to remain for the duration of the house party. I just wanted to warn you that I might leave on short notice. However, if you are involved with Windermere, I'll understand that you might wish to remain behind."

"Windermere was a fling and nothing more. You are my friend and we came together. If you wish to leave then so will I." Esme peered at Harriet's face closely when she winced. Her friend had parted with lovers before and never once showed regret or discomfort. In this case, though, it seemed she wasn't capable of keeping her feelings so well hidden. She was deeply upset and Esme thought she knew why. "Are you in love with him?"

After a long moment, her friend dipped her chin to confirm it. "I fear so."

She drew Harriet closer as her shoulders shook with silent sobs. A small wail of misery slipped out past her control as she vented her grief over the end of what had been a lengthy and often tempestuous affair. Harriet had never cried when an affair ended with her other lovers. Nor did Esme. They were alike in so many ways. Her friend would be better off without the blighter, and Lord Avery would undoubtedly move along to another conquest without hesitation.

She did her best to soothe her friend. "Then it is a good thing that you've broken with him. I cannot imagine it was easy sharing him with other women before. Even worse if you loved him."

Harriet straightened suddenly, pulling a polite mask over her emotions and broken heart. "Enough of my troubles. Tell me about Windermere. Did he make you happy?"

A small thrill raced through Esme and she worked hard to suppress it. "He is talented at making a lady feel rather special."

"Good. At least his reputation is deserved. I would not have you unhappy too." Her friend stood suddenly. "This might be cowardly, but I'm not quite the thing today. I'm going to make myself scarce. I will see you before dinner."

"You're not a coward. You just need a bit of time." Esme followed her to the door. "I am sorry about Avery, my dear."

"So am I." She let herself out and swiftly traversed the distance to her bedchamber down the hall.

Esme waited until Harriet's door closed behind her then closed hers slowly with a sigh.

There was always a danger in conducting intimate relationships that one party might grow to feel more than the other. So far, she had been lucky that her partners had never stirred her heart. Was she too particular about whom she loved?

She liked to think she was, and with good reason. She had never wanted any man to take her affections for granted. Her late husband had done that. Heathcote had turned to another the moment they'd both realized Esme would never bear his child. To this day, she could not forgive him for making her doubt her own worth. She wouldn't ever give a man that much of a hold on her emotions again. She enjoyed men but kept a distance.

After all, what was the point of falling in love with a man who would undoubtedly want children she couldn't have given him?

The life she had was the one she needed. Uncomplicated and undemanding of her emotions. She was happy as a widow. Indeed, she'd never missed being a wife.

With that thought in mind, she headed downstairs to enjoy tea on the terrace with people who had become dear friends since she'd learned to be happy on her own.

Chapter Seven

Richard scratched his jaw as undeniable satisfaction and conflicting confusion filled him with restlessness. How had he gone from arguing with a woman constantly to wanting to spirit her to his bed in the space of a few hours? He'd like to drag Esme away from his guests, over his shoulder if she became difficult about it, and make love to her all afternoon.

Admittedly, their encounter at the river house last night had been glorious and unplanned. The spur-of-the-moment decision to seduce her had been well-timed and swiftly executed.

But making love to her had been akin to holding fireworks. Dangerous and exciting, she was entirely capable of making a man's heart stop from the pleasure to be found in her passion. He'd known, of course, that Esme liked sex. She'd had no lack of lovers over the years since becoming a widow. For the life of him, he didn't understand why they hadn't been intimate long before this. When he looked at Esme for any length of time, his tension grew until, without a shadow of a doubt, he knew he would pursue an affair with her for as long as they could stand each other.

Last night had not been enough to quiet his need for her.

He was sorry she wouldn't ever have a child, but he wasn't fool enough not to take advantage of it. Since he didn't need to be careful where he spilled his seed, there was no reason not to indulge with her every chance he got. The house party ran for six more days and that would give him many opportunities to be alone with her. If she accepted his invitation to indulge in a purely intimate affair, that was.

He glanced across the terrace to where she sat among the women of the party, taking in the sun of another perfect country day. Outwardly, she seemed no different, but he remembered all too well how she had reveled in his attention last night. It astonished him how much she'd clearly enjoyed their hasty romp. Normally, he wasn't quite so aggressive with a new lover, but she hadn't seemed to mind his impatience.

Esme brought out the worst in him.

Or was it the best?

"Penny for your thoughts, old man," his brother remarked as he took a nearby chair, half-empty glass dangling from his fingers. On first glance, one might think Avery was merely tired, but his blue eyes were bloodshot and he seemed not altogether steady. He was completely cup shot, and very much earlier in the day than was normal for him during their usual house parties.

Richard had no interest in overindulging in spirits along with him. Not with Esme on his mind. "Is there a problem?"

"No. No problem." Avery chuckled. "But I had to come and see you. I've just been the recipient of the most astonishing bit of gossip from my valet."

Ah, the gossip. Richard was coming to regret the decision to allow his servants to spread tales that he and Esme had been intimate just to salvage her pride. "And what would that be?"

"Is it true you dabbled with the Lady Heathcote?" Avery stared pointedly across the terrace to Esme. "You risk your appendage to frostbite there."

He risked being scorched. The woman was wild and he certainly intended to explore every inch of her body, discover everything she liked most and do it to her repeatedly. He clenched his jaw, astonished how just thinking of fucking her caused his cock to thicken.

"I guess your distraction answers that question. Despite the temper, she is lovely?" Avery snorted. "When I saw the guest list, I must admit I was entirely taken aback. I thought she didn't like you. Didn't you two exchange strong words? Some claim it was a lover's tiff but I didn't believe it at the time."

They had frequently been at odds. But Richard would give their arguments entirely just to hear her moan his name again in the heat of passion over and over again. "She likes me enough."

That was also a problem. Despite becoming lovers last night, he had no idea how to go on with her. Esme had brushed aside suggestions to make a night of it and retired to her bedchamber alone last night. Richard had accepted but not liked her refusal terribly much, and had made a cursory circuit of his home before he too headed to his bed alone. They hadn't spoken this morning beyond common courtesies. Esme had immersed herself in conversation with the other guests and barely glanced his way after that. Normally, a lack of polite conversation with her wouldn't concern him, but he would give everything he owned to know how she viewed last night. And him.

The group Esme had been sitting with broke up and she excused herself from them to walk into the garden with Jillian. He tracked her movements, his body already awakening to the idea of a daylight tryst. A romp in a sun-filled glade with Esme would fill his mind with clearer images of the body he'd made love to last night. She was much softer than he'd imagined. Not weak but strong and flexible.

She and Jillian stopped to converse beside the fountain and he took a pace forward. Was Esme going to mention her disapproval of her relationship with Lord Hogan? He watched Jillian closely and although she did not seem outraged, she did grow more subdued during the conversation. Esme was upsetting her, but then they embraced and everything appeared to be congenial once more.

"Hmm, is that competition I see poised to take your place?" Avery mused, pointing toward the stables.

Albert Meriwether had paused in the shade of a tree, watching Esme and Jillian converse rather obviously. Since he appeared dressed for riding and hadn't been in sight all morning, Richard assumed he'd recently returned from visiting his new fiancée on her neighboring estate.

"He hasn't a chance," Richard insisted. "Married men, or about-to-be-married men, are not her type."

"Ah, is that why she settled for you last night?"

Richard bristled. The idea that he'd come second to Meriwether rankled. He chose to offer no comment. Avery would needle him no matter what he said to deny it anyway, and drunk, he'd be ten times as obvious to others.

"Better claim what's yours, brother, before someone else does. As I have learned, women are fickle creatures, every last one." Avery sighed. "She *is* lovely. Out of curiosity, just how adventurous in bed is she?"

"I have no idea yet but I intend to find out." He spun about and saw speculation in Avery's eyes. They had bedded the same lovers in the past but never at the same time. Usually before or after the other was done with them. But Esme and Avery? He couldn't bear that idea. "Do not even think of approaching her."

Avery winced and he drained his glass. "There's nothing

wrong with additional companionship in bed."

Richard scowled and shook his head. "I doubt Lady Ames' and Esme's friendship extends that far. Find someone else for a third, Avery."

"Fine. You can keep the little dragon." His brother scowled and stood. "But I'll do what I want with whoever I want."

Richard ignored Avery's belligerent tone and was grateful when his brother went on his unsteady way in an obvious huff. He tried to relax about Esme. They were nothing to each other really. One night with her warm body to play with should not make him feel so damned possessive. She was very good at hiding her real feelings behind a polite mask and his tension increased. When it came to Esme, looks were absolutely deceiving.

God help him, he'd never imagined he could feel so strongly about where Esme spent her time. She confused him, attracted him and yet with her, he was wary of putting a foot wrong. He was entirely without sense this morning and he didn't know what to do with himself—but watch her and wait for some sign that she might want him again.

Chapter Eight

A warm summer's day amused by friends had been just what Esme had really needed. Listening to their lives, their concerns and hopes for their families, brought a sense of inclusion to her life that a hundred balls never could. One could hardly talk candidly at a ball, there were too many ears and not enough friends among them, and she had much to say to one lady in particular.

Lady Jillian frowned. "And there are gentlemen like that?"

"Oh yes," Esme insisted, pulling Windermere's sister farther along the path and deeper into the garden. She was very glad to have a chance to talk to Jillian alone but she had to be delicate about how she'd come about her knowledge. "Many men enjoy taking a firm hand with women who like that sort of thing for pleasure. But believe me, Hogan is an out-and-out bully about it. Not the way a casual observer would notice, but it is there."

Esme kept her eyes on Jillian. The woman was still young; a widow who'd loved her older husband dearly. But by all accounts, she'd been utterly controlled by that man. Not cruelly but certainly kept as a possession. Rumor had it that Jillian's late husband had been a man with an extensive collection of sexual accoutrements designed for both pleasure and pain too. How far Jillian had enjoyed that life wasn't clear, but Esme suspected the woman was lost and without someone to talk to about her old life.

She squeezed Jillian's hand. "It will start out small, a gathering left early, a favorite dancing partner you will be pressured to refuse more often than not, a hat he doesn't like changed at the last moment. Over time, you would lose friends and disappoint your family by being so wrapped up in his concerns as to have no time for anyone else. You might not make any decisions without consulting him first just to keep pleasing him."

"But I always consulted my late husband."

"Not in everything I suspect." Esme sighed, thinking of how she'd failed one friend already in her life. She could not afford to be so timid again. Not where Hogan was involved. "I never noticed what Hogan did to Vera's life until it was far too late to make a difference."

"Who was she?"

"A neighbor in London whom I saw frequently, but not so often as every day. Luncheon invitations were the first to go, and then she was often not at home to me when I called, although I realize in hindsight that Hogan had likely told her not to receive callers. I allowed her to sever the acquaintance when I should have fought harder to stay involved in her life."

Jillian's brow creased. "What happened to her?"

"She died." Esme remembered that tragic day, and the events of the few before that she'd pieced together afterward. "When he broke it off abruptly after a row over her gloves, of all things, Vera was distraught and begged him to forgive her. She chased his carriage down the street and then collapsed in tears when he wouldn't stop. My servants and I helped her return home and that's when I discovered how much she'd changed. He'd made her so dependent on his opinion that in the end, when he refused to see her anymore, she chose to die rather than go on alone. He destroyed her confidence in herself, a little bit at a time, until there was nothing left to go on with."

"Oh," Jillian said, her face pale. "That's a tragedy."

"You must be careful of such men." Esme bit her lip and then sighed. She couldn't speak of this in half-truths forever if she wanted to spare Jillian future pain. She had to be blunt. "Benjamin Moore was very different. He treasured you. He had a way with you that excited your body, but he never forced you to change your mind. Never punished you because you chose kid gloves over silk. He used warning words, a secret language perhaps, to let you know what he wanted you to do for him and what he would do to you."

Jillian licked her lips and her eyes darted in all directions. Her breath came fast, undoubtedly panicked by Esme's knowledge of such matters. She took a pace backward. "How could you know so much about my husband?"

"I have been acquainted with men *like* him and their unusually dominating passions before," Esme murmured gently. "I have rarely been comfortable in a passive role, but for some women, and men too, a firm hand is bed play and beyond is required for their happiness. I believe you are such a woman, and I assure you there is nothing wrong with that."

All the air left Jillian's lungs and she sagged. "I'm so lost without Ben."

"I can see that, but you won't always be alone," Esme assured her, relieved the woman would confide in her. "You must be careful whom you reveal your true nature to and whom you trust. There are good men who can fill your needs without crushing your will into the bargain."

"Like who?"

"Like..." Did she really want to push Jillian into another

man's arms, control, so soon after losing her husband? Jillian undoubtedly needed time to grieve for Benjamin and decide if she wanted that life still. She could give the woman hope though. "The relationship you had depended on mutual respect and affection. That takes time. I could not in good conscience suggest any one man who could suit you. Only you can know what you need by spending time with them."

"You've given me much to think about." Jillian stared at her and then blushed. "When I married Ben, I did not know I was like this. For a long time I feared I was perverse."

Esme curled her arm through Jillian's again and led her along the path that would take them back to the house. "You are a good woman and deserve respect no matter how you find pleasure," she promised. "Do not rush into the next bed just because a man will say you must belong in him."

She had always liked Jillian. Although not a fixture in society, Esme had come to feel a deep affection for Windermere's sister from the few weeks they'd spent in each other's company over the years. Jillian was funny and kind and possessed a keen intelligence Esme couldn't bear to see harmed.

"I will do as you suggest and not rush. Thank you, Esme," she said with a smile. "My brother might think he's patching up your supposed rift but I am very glad you've come, if only to advise me. I might have made a terrible mistake with Lord Hogan."

Esme said nothing to that, but was very glad Jillian's eyes had been opened to the variety of men in the world, and the power she had in choosing one.

Jillian's gaze sharpened, focusing over Esme's shoulder. "I suppose I should be getting back to the housekeeper too. My brother's parties at least keep my mind occupied so I don't miss Ben so much. And I think a gentleman wishes to speak with you."

Esme rolled her eyes and turned, expecting to find Lord Windermere ready to berate her for warning Jillian off Lord Hogan—and instead found Albert Meriwether approaching, his stride determined as he bore down on them.

She squeezed Jillian's hand. "Do pass along my compliments to the housekeeper and staff too. Last night's ball was a wonderful success."

"They will be thrilled to hear you think so. The poor dears worry so." Jillian laughed softly. "I'll see you later for tea with Harriet."

"Of course." Esme affected an ease to hide her irritation when Meriwether bowed. "Mr. Meriwether. What an unexpected surprise. Glorious day, isn't it?"

The man smiled shyly. "Am I disturbing you?"

She had once thought his smile endearing, but now his manner annoyed her. She shrugged, glancing over her former lover and seeing him in an entirely new light. His affectionate nature hadn't truly increased with a longer acquaintance. What had she been thinking to believe a holiday together would bring them closer? It had done the exact opposite. He'd come here with an agenda that Esme played no part in. "Certainly not."

He drew closer. "I couldn't help but notice you seem very somber."

Talking with Jillian and speaking of Vera's tragic death had been a melancholy business, but such moments were short-lived. "I am in excellent spirits, as always," she told him. She gestured to the riding crop in his hands. "Are you just come from your fiancée's home?"

Meriwether shuffled his feet. "Oh yes, a pleasant luncheon with her family."

"Ah," Esme murmured, realizing how little she was affected by his news. Neither angry nor sad nor even disappointed in the situation. She didn't feel anything about the loss of her lover and his status as an engaged man. "You must be happy."

"I am." He suddenly frowned. "Despite my marriage, I hope we might remain friends and that you know you might always rely on me."

Esme blinked. "What could I possibly need to rely on you for? I am not in any distress. And I imagine your marriage will not increase our knowledge of each other to the point where a deeper friendship can develop."

"There's no reason we cannot remain on the best of terms." He drew near. "If we were discreet."

She narrowed her eyes. Did he assume she'd ignore the fact he was to marry? Men who did, placing so little importance on the commitment they'd made to another, were pitiful, in her opinion. The one thing she would never willingly do was usurp a wife's place in a husband's affections. They'd discussed marriage once too, her disinclination to wed again, but perhaps in the exuberance of his successful suit, he'd forgotten her prohibition on entanglements with married and engaged men. "There is every reason. Your future wife's feelings, for one. I will not be a party to breaking her heart."

Meriwether caught her hand in his. "Jane will be a dutiful wife."

"So I have heard." And that was from Lord Windermere. His praise of Jane had been a commonplace compliment at best. She removed her hand from Meriwether's clinging grip. Jane would be like any properly raised young woman in society today. She'd overlook her husband's wandering eye and if he strayed into another woman's bed, she'd hide her hurt from everyone. She would bear the insult in stoic silence, but Esme would never be the one to cause it. "Do give her my regards when you see her next and my best wishes for your happy marriage."

"That won't be for a few days. I had hoped to enjoy the

rest of the house party with you." He smiled a little too warmly. "We came with that intention and I apologize for being distracted."

He considered marriage a mere distraction? Good grief, he was cold! "My interest currently lies elsewhere," she assured the man.

He glanced behind him. "With our host?"

Esme was aware that Lord Windermere was watching her every move very closely this morning. Ordinarily, she could ignore him, but today her feelings were mixed. She didn't mind him looking, yet she didn't quite know how to react to him. Last night had been good between them. Surprisingly good, and she'd slept well afterward and awakened refreshed and invigorated. But considering the fact that she had been fielding discreet questions about her fling with Windermere all morning, and even this fool had noticed, she would have to speak to Windermere alone and have him stop being so obvious about his interest. "With whomever I choose. Good day, sir."

"I understand," he cried out urgently as she turned away. "You were angry with me last night. I forgive you."

Esme pivoted slowly, unable to hide her surprise. "I beg your pardon?"

"You must have been hurt very badly by last night's turn of events if you'd make the mistake of letting that man seduce you." Meriwether removed his hat and raked his fingers through his hair. "Things with Jane happened so fast and I know you were expecting me instead. There is no reason to share his bed again. I'm free to be with you until the end of the house party and when we return to London, I want to call on you at home as usual."

Anger surged through her. How dare he think her affair with Lord Windermere existed purely because she'd lost *him*. Windermere was not second-rate to anyone. He was as vigorous a lover as any she'd had, far more commanding than Meriwether in fact.

Esme pressed her fingers to her temple. *Dear God, am I about to defend Lord Windermere's prowess after a lifetime of disdain?* Apparently so.

She dropped her hand and straightened her shoulders. "Lord Windermere is a generous lover of great skill and expertise. I enjoyed *every* moment in his arms."

Meriwether's face leeched of color. "You couldn't mean that."

"Actually I do." She smiled thinly. "We are very much alike, Lord Windermere and I. And he understands me much better than it appears you do. I would never lower myself and sleep with a man whose affections are supposed to be engaged elsewhere. I chose him last night and will undoubtedly do so again. Excuse me."

Chapter Nine

Richard moved to the steps of the terrace, prepared to risk Esme's wrath by intervening in what appeared to be an argument between her and Meriwether. A burst of unexpected anger trickled through him that she'd been pushed so far as to be upset. The irony was not lost on him. Normally he was the one upsetting Esme, and that fact had never bothered him one bit in the past.

If Meriwether continued to aggravate Esme, he'd send him from the estate. The man had his chance with Esme and had thrown it away to marry the blandest debutante in the district.

Richard would not be so stupid.

After a moment, Esme headed toward the terrace steps and him. Although her face remained impassive, her steps were the clipped march of someone trying not to show her hurry. Richard had always been able to judge her anger fairly well. She was utterly furious.

Their eyes met and instead of caution, an unexpected jolt of lust struck him like a blow. Had he always been so affected by her or was it just because they'd been intimate once?

She stopped a pace away, near enough that he could reach out and haul her into his arms. He waited to see what she wanted first.

"Do you have a moment for private conversation, Lord Windermere?"

Gods, he hoped she wanted him for sex. He glanced at Meriwether and allowed a small territorial smile to spread over his face. "I am at your disposal immediately, my dear."

"Good."

She stepped around him and headed for a little-used entrance to his home through his open study doorway. Richard followed and, thinking she'd rather not have anyone overhear whatever came next, he closed and locked the doors. She was usually *very* expressive when angry, and even more so when she climaxed. "What did Meriwether say to you?"

As he turned, Esme pressed against him. "Enough of that fool." She caught his head with one hand and dragged his face to hers for a deep, hungry kiss. Her passion stole his breath away and it took him a moment to respond. Unfortunately, that hesitation seemed to build a fire in her. He was shoved roughly backward until he all but fell into his desk chair.

Esme hiked up her skirts and settled astride his lap without preamble. "I don't like to be stared at all the time."

Uncertain what to make of this development, he gently placed his hands on her bottom to secure her to his lap. "I did not mean to do it."

She made a little growl, much like a hungry cat on the hunt for an escaping mouse. She dug between them for the buttons of his trousers and practically ripped the garment open. When she slid her hand inside and curled her fingers around his cock, he groaned loudly.

Esme smiled wickedly and kissed him once. "Liar."

With her tongue dancing across his lips and her hot little hand working to bring him erect, Richard had no power to resist and certainly no desire to stop her. He jostled her to shove his trousers lower off his hips and then dug under her gown to touch between her legs.

He moaned at the state he found her in. "You might not *like* me staring but I think you are incredibly aroused by me doing it."

"I am frustrated."

He was glad to have made any impression today, so he chuckled and nibbled her neck, earning a gasp. "I can accommodate you," he whispered. "I can give you exactly what you need and more."

"You'd better." She rose up and Richard grasped his length so she could impale herself. She moaned as he filled her. "Yes."

He cupped her face, now flushed with heat and desire, and stared into her eyes, almost gray but rimmed by blue, he realized. She was incredibly kissable. "I'm starting to think you like me."

"Oh, be quiet." She closed her eyes and began to move.

Straddling his thighs as she was, it seemed a bit awkward at first to make love this way, so Richard grasped her hips to guide her. "Allow me."

He lifted and lowered her on his length, driving himself toward crazed very quickly. Esme was unlike other woman he'd made love to. She aroused him so easily and now that he had her wrapped around him once more, he never wanted the moment to end.

He met her gaze as they made love to each other. Esme rocked and ground her sex against him as if she too had fallen under a spell, oblivious to anything but the passion curling around them. Richard kissed her hard, thrusting his tongue into her mouth as he had last night and letting his hands fall from her hips so he could embrace her.

He needed her. Gods, he'd needed her for so long.

Esme continued her slow grind on his cock and he widened his legs a touch so she would have more of him. She groaned and buried her face against his neck. Her body quivered. "Oh, that's perfect."

Quickly, Richard touched her clitoris. The bud was large and when he rubbed it, Esme clutched him. She came apart with a sob muffled by his shoulder, quite unlike her throaty yell by the river last night but just as satisfying to his ears.

She lifted her head immediately, stared at him with dazed, heat-filled eyes and red, parted lips. Her pussy fluttered and squeezed around his length. When it happened again and again, he shuddered. If she could keep that up his release would be unavoidable. Her look alone would bring any man to his knees, but combined with her other talents he might not have any control where she was concerned.

Esme rose and he forced her back down as he filled her body with his seed on a hoarse shout.

Richard dragged her head to his shoulder again and she cuddled against him for a long moment while he caught his breath. "I must confess I'd hoped for another romp with you all morning, but that was entirely too quick. Maybe the chaise for a second round? As soon as I catch my breath I will carry you there and begin again properly."

"There's no need."

Esme abruptly extracted herself from his embrace while he sat in stunned silence, trousers around his thighs, cock softening and exposed. When Esme wasn't arguing with him, she was delightful in every respect. "I hadn't minded holding you. That was lovely."

Her expression when she looked at him was apologetic. "I don't normally do that."

He wanted to rejoice in her embarrassment but bit his lip to hold it in a moment longer. A flustered Esme was too amusing and rare. "Use men for sex when you're angry?"

She nodded and he let loose a hearty chuckle. "I didn't mind in the least," he assured her. "In fact, you could do that to me again and again and I'd never complain. Hopefully, next time I can last a little longer. I am grateful it wasn't me who irritated you so much though."

"You *did* irritate me. But it was something Meriwether said that provoked me to," she waved a hand in his direction, "do that."

"Oh." Richard stood and straightened his clothes. "What did the buffoon have to say for himself today?"

"He forgave me for falling for your charms and in the next breath assured me we could go on as usual when we return to London."

"As I said—a buffoon." Richard shook his head. "Your avoidance of married men is well known."

She considered him a long time and then her eyes sparkled with amusement at last. "I am very glad you understand that. You have to marry soon so this must end before then."

"Agreed." He observed Esme. Intelligent, passionate, a perfectly poised woman in any situation, including arguments. Yes, passion with Esme was all very fine, but was anything more, deeper, out of the question?

He smiled at her as an idea took hold. "What would you say to a second romp out of doors? Are you adventurous enough to risk other people seeing us together in a compromising position?"

An excited gleam filled her eyes but then dimmed just as quickly. "Not today. I promised to meet with your sister and Harriet very soon."

Disappointment filled him and then acceptance. He could wait. "Well, perhaps tomorrow you might come riding with me in the morning. There are a few things changed from your visit last year. I'd like to show you around the rest of the estate since you so clearly enjoy telling me what to do with my affairs." He smirked just to annoy her.

She brushed aside his remark with a wave of her hand. "I'm sure your guests would enjoy the tour."

"Just us, Esme. I would explore this peace between us

fully while it lasts."

She frowned then. "We can end things if you prefer. You should not neglect your guests."

"Not yet." He grinned and caught hold of her fingers. "Not when there is so much pleasure to be had with you. I should ask, rather than assume: Would you consider being mine for what remains of the house party?"

The corner of her mouth lifted into a wicked smile he'd grown to crave. She reached to his waist and, to his surprise, secured a button that had come undone on his waistcoat. "Well, I suppose I could tolerate your attentions a little longer."

He smiled broadly and drew her into his arms one last time and nuzzled her neck, earning a gasp from her. Yes, definitely another bout was required today to dull the ache of want already returning. Perhaps they could meet tonight. "What if I come to regret this bargain of ours and want a longer affair?"

She drew back, hands rising to straighten his cravat into neat folds. Had he been that ruffled as to need his valet? Esme appeared utterly impeccable despite what they'd done on his chair. "I like a man who can keep his word."

"I can." But it would be so easy to continue to explore their mutual passion. He brought her fingers to his lips and kissed each one. "My bedchamber or yours tonight?"

Her eyes flickered over his body. "Yours, but only so I might lie surrounded by Jillian's beautiful art. That is the only reason to visit your room again."

"Liar." He kissed her lips, hard and greedily, anticipation for tonight's adventure consuming him all at once. He smiled. "But a lovely one. You want me, admit it."

She gifted him with a smile. "Perhaps I do. You show *some* talent."

He laughed hard at that and sent her on her way before he proved on his settee just how talented he could be.

Chapter Ten

As Adrian and Carolyn Hill rode away, back toward the manor house and guests, Esme scowled at Windermere. "Why do you invite them to your estate if you don't wish to spend time with them?"

"I invite them so she can visit with her family."

She frowned. "They haven't left the estate."

"Yes, I've noticed. My cousin is too busy dragging his wife from pillar to post furthering his acquaintance, from everyone in attendance at the balls to the tenant farmers."

She had noticed that last night too, and wondered why the man was cozying up to so many of Windermere's friends. She chose her next words with care. "Is it my imagination that Mr. Hill acts as if this will all be his one day?"

Windermere's mount pranced and he took a moment to calm the animal. "He can wait until we're dead first," he bit out savagely.

Esme was surprised by the display of anger. "I didn't suggest I agreed that he should."

Richard stared at her and then shook his head. "Forgive me. I know I shouldn't react but I've had it up to my ears with his hints and suggestions for how things should be done. Let's ride."

He kicked his mount ahead and Esme followed, her mare keeping pace with Windermere's larger beast fairly well. She enjoyed riding here. The vistas were beautiful, the air fresh and clean. A far cry from the pace and stench of London.

To be honest, she hadn't found anything about this visit that she'd have different, save for having to look at Meriwether over the dinner table each night. She'd been blind to his faults, his ambition to marry into the *ton* and elevate his family to new heights. It had become obvious to her now when she considered the matter with a calmer head that Meriwether had chosen a young woman who'd grant him what she couldn't: a way into the best circles *and* the offspring she could never have.

However, once she wasn't looking at her former lover, Esme didn't think of him again until the next meal came around. But she would never let such a situation happen to her again, and would choose her future lovers with more care and consider their likely ambitions before becoming intimately involved.

Windermere eventually reined in, a fair distance from the manor. He turned his mount in a wide arc and then fell in beside her. "Discussion of the succession annoys me."

"I did notice that." She cleared her throat. "You don't need me to suggest what must be done."

"I must marry." His grip tightened noticeably on the reins. "I know it."

At his age, he'd better marry soon. "Do you want my advice or should I keep my thoughts to myself?"

He glanced at her with a smile. "I'd rather hear them today than be surprised later."

"Lady Alice Beauchamp."

His brows shot up. "Who is that?"

"She is a widow, a mother of two small girls. She has a

passing acquaintance with your sister and is very kind and responsible. She might be young, but she has proven herself as a wife and mother."

He stared at her for a long time. "By bearing daughters?"

"Yes," Esme murmured, remembering the quiet little girls she'd met during the season. Windermere needed a son though. "The getting of an heir is up to fate unfortunately and cannot be predicted, but while her fortune is of no great consequence, her connections are excellent. She has the makings of a perfect countess for you."

The man at her side grunted. "What happened to her husband?"

"A riding accident." She winced. He did not appear happy with her choice or suggestion or the subject under discussion, but he had asked for her opinion. "Beauchamp's death was sudden and her year of mourning ended some time ago."

"I see. How well do you know her?" he asked.

"Enough to wish her a better future than her present."

"All right, I'll bite." He turned in the saddle, one hand on his hip. "What is that supposed to mean?"

"She lives with her husband's parents. The second son will inherit and she's looked upon I think as if she's let them down. The second son mocks her openly. I do not like that."

Windermere fiddled with the reins. "I'll think about it. After the house party."

After their affair ended was the meaning she heard behind his words. She would be sorry when their time was up, actually. She had enjoyed his attentions a great deal the past few days. They hadn't argued, but the time they spent together was filled with tension of a different sort. A pleasant excitement that never failed to arouse her.

After she left his estate, after the house party, she would

have to make sure she never lapsed into foolish nostalgia because she felt certain she would remember every intimate detail of him.

He turned into the forest, and she let the matter of whom to wed drop. It really wasn't her business when or who he married, but Lady Alice Beauchamp was a nice young woman who'd already proven herself in childbirth. The woman would be a good candidate if he'd but listen to her suggestion and make a wise choice this time around.

Esme held her mare in check when it would have followed him and stared across the valley behind her. To her left, farmland patched the valley floor and to the right, dense woodland stretched up to the highest peaks. The estate was a well-run enterprise with no loss of beauty or hardship for those who lived here. Behind her back was the forest marking the eastern border. Windermere kept his own woods sacrosanct and it had been rare he suggested a guest venture there, so she was doubly sure to enjoy such a boon.

She enjoyed the view a time alone then urged her mare to follow him into the dark wood. The trail appeared to take them far away from prying eyes and into a world of dappled light and quiet sound.

Windermere had waited for her a short distance in. He turned slightly in his saddle to see her. "Ride slowly," he advised. "The branches are low in places and I'd not like you hurt."

She lifted her brows. "Such a gallant gentleman."

He grinned. "Compliments so early in the day? But it's only eleven, Esme."

"Ungrateful rogue," she teased, with only half her heart in the rebuke.

Her breath caught as the real world fell far behind them. After a short ride, Windermere dismounted and led his horse toward a rough-hewn stone enclosure, almost a ruin. The place was likely private enough that no one would stumble upon the horses for some time.

She remained in her sidesaddle, watching him tend his horse with experience and familiarity in every movement. He was in his element, running away from his responsibilities and his guests to play with her. The idea of it pleased her immensely, if only briefly.

He came back to her grinning. "We'll walk from here."

"Where are we going?"

"Somewhere I've never taken anyone else."

She leaned forward onto her knee. "Should I be honored?"

"If you like." He caught her about the waist and lowered her to the forest floor, then stole a long, hungry kiss from her lips. He teased into her mouth with his tongue, feeding the desire that lingered when he was near. She was breathless when he drew back and then he smiled, one brow rising over his striking blue eyes. *Far too handsome for his own good.*

He took the reins from her, tended to her horse then secured both mounts in the small space. She frowned at the meager barrier.

"Don't worry," he said, reading her mind. "They're used to being left here and will remain calm until we return."

He held out his hand and she slipped hers into it. "I am very intrigued, Windermere."

"I hope so."

They walked a further ten minutes through pristine woodland, though following a well-trod path that she could never see the end of. "Others must come here."

"The family does, and some tenants if they've the stamina for the climb."

She glanced at the canopy of leaves above her head, but couldn't see the peaks above. "Are we going up the mountains today?"

"No, we're here. Almost."

The rush of water greeted her, a fast-flowing stream,

tumbling over mossy rocks not far ahead. Windermere guided her to the stream and then away. They squeezed between two trees grown close together and her heart lightened immediately.

"Oh my." He'd led her to a clearing, a grassy field protected by tall trees where the sun shone brightly through the gap in the canopy around them. "Heaven?"

"Very close to it," he murmured as he stripped off his gloves and shoved them in his pockets.

She was drawn to the center and spun about in a slow circle. A tight feeling began in her chest and she set her hand over her heart. "I knew your home was beautiful but *this* I never expected to find hidden away."

Windermere strolled toward her, dropped the blanket he'd carried and caught her face between her hands. "As beautiful as you. Are you done communing with nature alone?"

"Perhaps never," she whispered, heart pounding at the wicked gleam in his eyes. Windermere removed her gloves and drew a straight line from the tip of her longest finger to her wrist. She swayed toward him a little.

"I'll tempt you away somehow." He kissed her, slid his fingers into her hair and held her against him tightly. When the kiss broke, he brushed her cheek with his. "I'll spread the blanket."

He chose a spot with a slight incline and removed his coat, waistcoat and footwear. He patted the space at his side. "We won't be disturbed here. Come and lie down with me."

Then he tugged his cravat undone and left it dangling around his neck. He stretched out on the ground, sprawling on his back, his gaze locked on the patch of blue sky above them without a care in the world.

Esme considered her surroundings a moment more. They were very alone and unlikely to be stumbled upon. She removed the dark-red jacket of her riding habit, and on a whim stepped out of the heavy skirt too. She stood in corset and shift beneath a soft undershirt but kept her footwear on, letting the sun bathe her in light and warmth. When she joined Windermere on the blanket, his eyes were fixed on her body. She held herself away from him and stretched her limbs.

The peace of the place enveloped them. After a time, birds darted overhead, moving from tree to tree, the stream bubbled off in the distance. But nothing else moved or caused sound to be made. It was as if they were the only two humans in existence. She found Windermere's hand and held it. "How long can we stay?"

"An hour. A day. Forever." He smiled lazily. "I'm in no rush to leave."

His words, although certainly not intended that way, caused her pulse to jump. He made her think of intimacy and sex and his grasping hands no matter where they were or what they were supposed to be doing. Making love to him came so very easily and as she lay on the forest floor, an undeniable surge of anticipation filled her. She wanted him. She always seemed to want him the moment they were alone.

Windermere rolled toward her at the same moment she rolled toward him. They kissed again, lazy brushes of lip that set her body trembling. He cupped her breast and then dragged her close against his body. With the warmth of the sun and the scent of nature filling her lungs, her desire doubled.

She'd always enjoyed the outdoors but rarely enjoyed it half dressed.

Esme pushed Windermere onto his back and then straddled his lap, determined again to bend him to her will. Windermere slowly unfastened his trousers, pushed them down his legs and met her gaze. His cock was full, hard already.

"I need you," she whispered.

"I need you too."

He smiled as she moved to mount him. Her body was ready and moist and she ached in lovely places. The slide of his heat into her core sent a moan tumbling from her lips. "That's what I want," she whispered.

"On top again?" Windermere squeezed her bottom with both hands. "Ride me then, Essy."

She overlooked the shortening of her given name. She had overlooked half a dozen things he had done in the last days that had previously annoyed her. All so she might make love to him again.

She let him slide in and out of her body, teasing herself, fulfilling her deepest desires to have her way. It had been rare to make love outdoors too. She'd never been this entirely private with a man outside and relished the sheer indulgence. She made good use of the occasion and expressed her pleasure openly, loudly.

She pleased herself, pleased her own body's astonishing craving for Windermere. She made her pussy ache, shoving him deep then holding him at her entrance. She rotated her hips and ground down onto him until she could take no more. And still it wasn't enough. She was still hungry for him.

She met his gaze and saw his eyes were wide, brow coated with sweat. His fingers dug into her thighs as she slid up and down his length. She was torturing him, exciting him. She couldn't deny he did the same to her.

"Tell me what you want," he whispered.

"I want to hear your voice." She caught the ends of his cravat where it lay on his chest and tugged him up. "Tell me how you feel."

He rolled up, one hand slipping between her legs, the other sliding over her rump. His panting breath tickled her ear. "I would fuck you three times an hour if I could manage it. I would spread you over my lap, everywhere in my home, and possess you. I want my mouth on you, my cock in you at the same time. Dear God, I've never been with someone who made me feel so alive, so bloody eager. It's like I'm sixteen again and with my first woman."

He squeezed her bottom again and she gasped. She tightened her grip on his cravat, using it as a tether, as reins as she rode him.

He teased the bud of her clitoris with firm, fast strokes.

She came undone suddenly. Caught unprepared, she screamed his name even as he shouted hers.

The shocks of her climax continued to roll on and on until Esme was left shaking and weak.

Richard caught her as she fell boneless into his arms, her grip on his cravat loosening. He eased her to the blanket with such gentleness that she closed her eyes. She had not experienced a release like that in her entire life and she hadn't been prepared for the rush that had swept over her. She wanted to hold on to the feeling, the blinding contentment enveloping her, forever and never return to earth.

"What the devil?" Windermere exclaimed when she did not stir. He slapped her cheek very gently. Once, twice.

On the third, she opened her eyes and laughed at him. "I still breathe."

He sucked in a sharp breath. "Did you just black out?"

Had she? "No, but I believe I've been to heaven and back in the space of a few perfect moments."

His brows rose. "Perfect?"

"Oh, don't let it go to your head."

Unfortunately, he puffed out his chest. "I am very pleased madam is so thoroughly satisfied with me."

She stared at him a moment then covered her face with both hands. "Gods, I thought you would be smug but that smile is beyond reason."

"I'm satisfied too, you know. I did not know it would be like this. This good between us."

"Well, now you do." She lowered her hands slowly, just

a little bit proud of herself as well. "Don't ever doubt me again."

He brought her hand to his lips and kissed her knuckles. "Never, ever again."

He pressed a kiss to her breast as he rolled away to lay flat on his back and watch the sky above. He caught up her hand again and held it tightly within his. "What will I do after the house party?"

She shaded her eyes with one arm, wondering the same thing. "There's always another set of breasts, Windermere."

And there would be other men for her too.

"True, but the rest of the lady matters, as you've just proved to me." He kissed the back of her hand reverently once more. "I'll return shortly."

Esme lowered her arm from her eyes to watch him walk away, hitching his trousers up as he went and fastening them. Her heart skipped a beat. She would be sorry to lose him as a lover but it was inevitable. He needed a wife who could give him babies and she never dabbled with married men.

For an affair he was possibly perfect, but the rest she could never hope to have.

Chapter Eleven

—◆—

Esme gritted her teeth a moment before responding to the insult her lover's brother had just delivered very loudly to a crowded room. "Lord Avery, your compliments take my breath away."

For the life of her, she couldn't fathom why Lord Avery Hill had taken a set against the world tonight, but he'd grown particularly cutting toward her in the last few minutes.

"Wasn't a compliment," Avery slurred, the effects of his indulgence in spirits very obvious in the way he formed words. "Dragons need slaying and my sword is at the ready, ill-tempered wench."

The hovering crowd of guests sucked in a collective breath and the ladies began twittering behind their fans. Esme shook her head at their whispers. Avery was not always a nice man. Somewhat belligerent and entirely too sure his way was right, and they occasionally locked horns over his attitude that women were nothing more than disposable pleasures. Esme would weather whatever insults he threw out well enough, but the small crowd would remember every word he said and spread the news all over London.

"I'd say you fit that description better than I." She studied Avery with growing annoyance. He had already offended three other ladies tonight, made a pass at more than one servant, and refused to take himself somewhere more private to continue his drinking.

And after such a satisfying ride with Windermere, and their tryst under the warm summer sun earlier, Avery's attitude threatened to suck all the joy out of her day.

Unfortunately Windermere was nowhere to be found, and since Oswin and Lady Jillian appeared helpless to control Avery, Esme could see no choice but to step in and save the evening from total ruin. "If you could lead the others away," she whispered to Lady Jillian. "You might leave him to me."

Both Lady Jillian and the butler frowned at her request.

She smiled reassuringly to both. "I know exactly what to do with him. Trust me."

Lady Jillian bit her lip a moment, torn but too timid to take charge herself. "You do not mind?"

"Never fear. I grew up around belligerent men."

Jillian kissed her cheek. "I will owe you for this."

"And I promise to collect one day," she returned halfheartedly before she ushered Jillian and the milling guests toward the door. Best not to have Lord Avery utter any further scurrilous *opinions* on her character to others. If he didn't like her, so be it. But why he chose tonight to tell the whole world was disappointing.

The butler hovered at the doorway, dragging his feet in leaving. "I should stay," he offered.

The faithful retainer appeared so concerned that Esme shook her head firmly. Better to have the older man elsewhere in case Avery's attitude worsened. "Make sure everyone else is comfortable, Oswin," Esme advised, and then slowly closed the door in his face.

She knew how to handle men like Avery Hill. Her mother had died young and her brothers and father had been fond of drink in the years after. It had always been left to Esme to clean up the mess and right the furniture they'd knocked over as well as soothe ruffled feathers when she'd lived at home with them. Men often thought they were so clever, but a little gentle persuasion tended to go a long way.

She turned around and squared her shoulders. Avery followed her movements about the room through hooded eyes. He had made quite a mess and she straightened a few things back as she remembered them being positioned.

"Why are you still here?" He scowled. "Get out too. Stay away from me. I'm not going to poach on my brother's preserve."

Esme rolled her eyes at his contrary statements. "*As if that were possible*. A man of your appetites leaves me quite cold, I assure you."

His face darkened with anger. "I wouldn't touch you with a ten-foot pole."

"Say what you like to me, but I've always thought it preferable not to offend absolutely everyone at a house party when it's only halfway done." She smiled. "I sent the others away so you might enjoy keeping some friends for tomorrow and not completely embarrass your brother and poor sister."

"You can't tell me what to do," Avery hissed. "Just because my sainted brother got under your skirts doesn't mean you're on your way to becoming mistress of this house."

She burst out laughing at the mention of her fling with Windermere leading to a permanent situation between them. "Oh, my word, you must be foxed. I have a certain interest in your brother for the moment but I've no right or desire to keep him about for long, nor he me. In fact, I don't believe I've ever entertained the idea before, but I do thank you for the amusement."

"Harridan."

She reached for the bottle at his side and lifted it to her nose. "Gin. How very common of you."

"It does the job. Damn Oswin hid the wine cellar key from me again," he grumbled, sprawling deeper into the chair, holding a silver tankard at a clumsy angle in his fingers. Avery was so far gone he hadn't noticed he'd run out. A little more spirits in him and hopefully he'd pass out and that would be the end of him for the night. Esme grinned at the idea, steadied his hand, and refilled the tankard halfway.

Avery stared at the mug a moment. "My thanks. At last, a woman who knows what a man needs without having to talk a subject to death."

When he lifted it to his lips to drink, a fair portion escaped to slide down his jaw and the chair beneath him. Esme shuddered as the cushion grew damp and ruined from his spillage. The chair, the pattern particularly, was one of her favorites. She might not be mistress of this house, but she appreciated the beauty around them more than Lord Avery Hill ever could.

"Such a mess again," she chided. "Beyond last year's efforts, indeed. I'll never understand why Harriet put up with you. She should have found someone who wouldn't embarrass her with the way you go on."

"I fuck well." Avery saluted her with his tankard. "Good luck to her finding a replacement that makes her scream like I can in bed."

For added clarity, he lewdly grabbed his groin with his spare hand, but it was easy to tell that what lay beneath his clothing was in no condition to live up to his boast.

"I'm sure there will be dozens of men who vie for her attention when we return to London," she replied in a bored tone but watched him for a reaction. He winced and then wiped the expression clean. Esme sat across from him. "But is that all you do with her?"

Avery swallowed a large mouthful and then wiped his

sleeve across his lips. "I've had dozens of women in my bed. They've never complained about my techniques."

She knew his history and of his skill with women, thanks to Harriet's shared confidences. "They've little chance of complaining since after sharing your bed, you barely see any of them again," she muttered under her breath. "But you always kept coming back to Harriet before she could find someone better."

He squinted as if he'd stopped listening. "Eh?"

"Oh, nothing." She would laugh aloud at how slow-witted Avery was under the influence of spirits, but this was the man her best friend had fallen for. If he had any sense, he'd be trying to mend fences with Harriet rather than drowning his sorrows that he'd lost her through his own actions. The safest thing for all concerned was to get him into his own bed, alone, and perhaps tomorrow he'd be a touch more civilized, at least enough to apologize to those other offended ladies. "Have you had enough?"

"Keep out of my affairs." Avery hugged his tankard against his chest, slopping more onto his shirt. He glared into the cup, and then drained every last drop in one swallow. Afterward, he swayed forward to show her the empty tankard. "I can hold my liquor."

"Is that so?" From years of Harriet's confidences and Esme's own observations, she knew he actually couldn't. Her plan was working so well. "Well then, let me refill that for you, my lord, and you can prove to me how fine a gentleman you really are."

She refilled the tankard to the brim and then sat back to watch him drink in peace. All too soon the man could barely find his mouth.

He jerked upright suddenly. "Do you know what that woman wants?"

His sudden question surprised her, but Esme assumed "that woman" referred to her friend Harriet. "She wants what we all want."

"Excitement. A bit of fun." He scowled. "I gave her a damn good time."

Esme shook her head. "You haven't a clue about women, do you?"

He stared, and then smoothed his damn shirtfront. "More of an idea than my sainted brother."

"Now, *that* is where you are wrong." She sighed. "All we want is a man who will put our needs first."

"There, you see," he said with a renewed burst of energy. "I always wait for her."

Of course his mind ran to sex but that wasn't what she'd meant. "I'm not speaking of intimacy, but I fear you are too blinded by drink to understand the difference at the moment."

He lurched toward her, falling to his knees in his haste. "Tell me."

Esme pushed him away with the tips of her fingers and he collapsed onto the floor in an untidy heap.

He squeezed his eyes shut. "Gave her every pleasure I could think of."

He groaned and rolled away, curling onto his side, almost in a ball, resting his head on his arm like the most innocent babe. But this man wasn't at all innocent and he hardly deserved her sympathy for the way he lived his life.

Esme prodded his shoulder with the toe of her shoe after a long moment of silence from him and received no response. She sat back and regarded him sadly. "Fool. All she wanted was your undivided attention."

He snored suddenly and her heart ached for Harriet. She knew very well what her friend had wanted most of all and had given up. What she wanted would never be possible with Avery unless he was prepared to change his life completely. "She wanted your love, Avery. That is all a woman really needs to be happy."

Chapter Twelve

———— ✦ ————

"**H**ow the hell did this happen?" Richard shook his head in disgust as he stared at the body at his feet. His brother was passed out and drooling on the damn rug in the little sitting room just off the ballroom.

An appalling thought struck him. His brother wasn't a good drunk. Too mouthy by far, too rude to all and sundry. Richard had been occupied in the stables for hours so he'd have had plenty of time to cause trouble. "Oh God. Do I need to make amends to anyone in particular tonight?"

The butler winced. "He spoke rudely to several ladies until Lady Heathcote intervened. Lady Jillian has smoothed the other ladies' ruffled feathers I believe but an apology from your brother might be in order."

Richard winced. Esme took offense quite easily to the things he said and he didn't want to imagine her mood over his brother's rudeness. An upset would affect his hopes for the rest of the house party. "I'll speak to Lady Heathcote and the others myself tonight."

"Actually, when the countess left your brother, she didn't seem particularly offended by events," Oswin remarked. "She merely asked me to lock him in as he was and to wait for your instructions. She returned to the other guests quite happily, I feel. When I saw her last, she was laughing with Mr. Hammond on the terrace."

Unease filled him at the idea of Esme and Hammond laughing together while he'd been stuck out in the stables attending to urgent estate business. He studied his brother and then glanced at the clock. Almost two in the morning and the house party was only just winding down for the night. The whole time he'd been in the stables, he hadn't been imagining Esme dealing with his brother, or smiling and laughing with someone else. He'd foolishly hoped she'd been wondering where he'd gone.

His brother snored on, uncaring for the difficult position he was likely in. Richard wasn't sure what was going on with Avery, but he'd have to get him upstairs and into his bed. He hoped there wasn't a woman waiting because Avery was in no condition to make any sort of good impression. "Do you know who is sharing my brother's bed at the moment?"

The butler nervously glanced around. "I don't believe there is anyone this year."

Richard frowned. "Surely Lady Ames?"

"Not currently." The butler dug a finger beneath his neckcloth, clearly discomforted by the topic of their discussion.

It was accepted there was often more than one woman sneaking from his brother's bed at any time of the day or night. Until now, Richard had never needed to discuss those peculiarities with his butler.

Oswin glanced around quickly to make sure they were still alone before continuing, "The maids say Lady Ames broke with Lord Avery. Quite upsetting for her. She's kept to her room tonight, I am afraid to say."

Oswin glared at the body on the floor.

"And my brother has been drunk since yesterday morning." Richard groaned. "A lover's tiff. That explains everything. When will he learn not to lead women on?"

Oswin cleared his throat. "Might I ask about your interest in Lady Heathcote?"

"My interest?" He glanced at his butler in surprise. "Of what concern is that to you? You are not her father."

"No, but I felt compelled to inquire, given the care she has shown to me during her many visits." Oswin lifted his chin proudly. "She is a good woman and her influence on you has been noted and approved of by your staff and tenants."

"I see." Richard blinked, blindsided by the fact that his staff had made so much of Esme's visits. "That is unexpected."

"The nursery has been empty for a long time," Oswin said, smiling awkwardly. "It would be nice to hear the voices of the very young at all hours of the day and night and to have a woman of her strength of character once more commanding us. We all agree on this."

The entire staff had placed their stamp of approval on Esme? It was too much. He scowled at the man he'd depended on to run his home. "My relationships are none of your business, not anyone's, Oswin, and you'd do well to remember your position here. Anyone can be replaced."

"Yes, my lord." However, Oswin looked anything but abashed. The man had meant his endorsement of Esme.

Richard turned away, shaking his head. He nudged his brother with the toe of his boot and got no response that could be considered intelligent communication. "I'll need some help getting him upstairs."

A throat cleared. Richard glanced over his shoulder and spotted Mr. Hammond hovering at the door. He breathed a sigh of relief to discover Esme was not at his side. She would not appreciate the conversation he'd just had.

Hammond drew close, scowling at the man on the floor. "I wouldn't trust me not to drop him on his head, but I am willing to take his feet."

"Thank you." Richard appreciated the offer of help.

"I've always found that a tempting thought too, to drop him. He never could handle the drink."

With Hammond's help, and a great deal of grunting, they got him up the back stairs, awkwardly thrown onto his bed still in the clothes he was wearing. He stank of gin, but there was no help for leaving him that way. Avery slept through it all, heavy as stone and just as sensible. It wasn't worth anyone's time to try to undress him.

Hammond lingered a moment. "Stupid fool. You'll never know what you had in her."

Richard frowned at his remark, uncertain if the man was speaking to him or his inebriated brother. "I beg your pardon?"

The other man smiled tightly. "Never mind. Good night, one and all."

He strolled out and disappeared quickly down the hall. Richard took one last look at his brother then closed the door to the room. Tomorrow he'd talk to Avery and find out what was going on. But tonight he needed to ensure Esme wasn't upset.

He hurried to her bedchamber and tapped lightly on her door, hoping Hammond hadn't left Windermere only to join her there.

"It's open," she called out.

He glanced around as soon as he stepped through, relieved to find she had not taken up with Hammond or anyone else in his absence. She was curled up in the window seat, an empty sherry glass in hand, her bare toes peeking from beneath her robe-covered nightgown. She was entirely too kissable like this and he hurried across the room.

She screwed up her nose when he got close. "Oh, it's you."

His hopes died. Had she not wanted him to come? "Were you expecting someone else?"

"No, but I thought to catch sight of you sooner than

this."

He slowly approached her. "One of the horses foaled tonight. I had wanted to be there."

Her expression cleared. "A filly or colt."

"Colt."

She turned to glance out the open window. "Congratulations."

Esme's greeting was not terribly warm and his tension grew. "I apologize for my brother's behavior if he has upset you. He seems very drunk."

She leaned her head back on the wall and studied him. "I know. I confess I helped him along until he passed out."

The news was somewhat of a relief. "He was rude to you."

When she said nothing more, Richard quickly squeezed into a spot by her feet. He placed his hand on her calf and softly stroked her limb through the robe. "Is everything all right?"

Her smile was tight. "Of course."

"Are *we* all right?"

"We?" She shook her head. "Windermere, we've enjoyed a few exciting trysts that have nothing to do with anything else. Your brother cannot affect my enjoyment of you no matter how drunk or uncivilized he becomes."

He shoved her robe aside to touch bare skin. "It's far more than sex between us and you know it." He skimmed his fingers up the back of her leg and higher still, until he could feel the damp heat of her quim.

Her legs parted on a sigh. "Very good sex indeed."

He stared at where his fingers played. Tonight, he wanted Esme in his bed completely naked for what remained of the night. "I hoped you might be amenable to joining me in my room."

She moved her hips closer to his fingers. "You're here. Why stop?"

He frowned. "I really do walk in my sleep."

"Oh." She glanced around swiftly, taking stock of the room with widened eyes. "Entirely too many breakable items?"

"Yes." He swallowed and teased her curls again. "This would be an easy room to hurt myself in. I had hoped to make a night of it. To exhaust us both."

"I would hate to see your blood on the carpets. These are lovely and your brother has already spoiled one chair with gin. A pity, that. You should make him clean up after himself tomorrow, and perhaps he would stop burdening your staff with extra work at a time like this."

He grinned at how no matter what he did to her body, her managing tendencies remained unaffected. No wonder his staff liked her. With Esme, he always knew what she expected.

He held out his hand. "I might just suggest it. It's about time he took responsibility for his actions and settled down."

After a moment, she slipped her small hand over his and he brought her to her feet. They stood next to each other, barely touching but his pulse sped. He bent to kiss her cheek then guided her toward the door.

In the hall, she faced him. "Did you leave your brother snoring below stairs?"

"Hammond and my butler assisted me getting him into his room. It was a near thing for all of us. We each wanted to drop him on his head, I think. I cannot help but worry about him." He glanced at Esme in time to see a dark expression form on her face. "Esme, do you know what's amiss?"

She waited until they stood outside his bedchamber before answering. "Perhaps."

"Lady Ames is upset." At her obvious surprise, he shrugged. "I don't always wait for you to tell me everything I need to know. My servants advise me of small tidbits of gossip from time to time during the house party. I am sorry. I hope my brother hasn't been an utter beast to her."

"It's more than that."

He blinked. "What else is there?"

Her frown grew. "Another time."

She slipped into his bedchamber and before the door was properly locked, she slipped off her robe. As was his usual habit, Richard crossed the room and slid the room key under his dressing-room door. "Don't be alarmed. My valet will unlock the chamber at half-five, long before the guests awake. You'll have ample time to return to your room unseen."

He faced Esme and his eyes widened. She was already undressed, slowly stroking her own breast. Her lips curved upward at his shock. She clearly enjoyed surprising him every way she could.

He hardened immediately, the stirring of desire he'd experienced earlier roared into impatience to have her again. Three strides placed him directly before her. He didn't dare touch her but admired the pert breast she caressed. He let his gaze rove over her deliciously pink skin, taking in every dimple, every curve, and growing even more aroused by what he found before him. "You have the figure of a young woman."

The wicked sparkle dimmed from her eyes. "The only advantage of never being blessed with children."

Her mention of children brought out a keen desire to see her body big with child. His. He almost groaned out loud as he imagined a life with Esme as his wife. Could she be happy with him and him alone?

He gently touched her head, slipping his fingertips into her silky hair.

He brushed his lips against hers slowly, keeping their first kiss light and gentle. The delicious scent of Esme's arousal curled around him and before he realized it, Richard had her cuddled into his chest, her fingers digging into his shoulders through his clothes as they held each other close.

He lowered one hand to her shoulder and circled his thumb over the delicate skin of her collarbone, finding her softness compelling. But it was her strength of character he'd grown to adore, and not just the sex that kept him coming back for more.

Against his lower back, Esme's touch was light as a feather, skimming his waist and quickening his heart with the relentless torture. He backed her toward the bed, but stumbled as his trousers slid down his legs and tangled about his knees.

He glanced down in surprise. Esme had undone them and he'd not noticed. The minx.

Her smile was rather smug, so he released her to finish undressing himself. "I take it you want me naked too?"

"I do." Esme circled him slowly, her fingertips skimming his stomach, his hip, gliding over the muscles of his arms and chest, teasing across the swells of his bottom before she stood before him again. "Much better."

Richard caught her up in his arms and held her against him. "Definitely, my sweet."

"Sweet?" She scoffed.

"Would you prefer to be called a feisty wench instead?"

"Oh, yes." She grinned then laughed softly. "I'm no milksop madam."

The smooth slide of her slender body against his increased the urgency to join with her. Instead, he lowered her to the bed, rolled her onto her stomach and kissed both cheeks of her bottom. Next, he whacked the right one.

"Windermere," Esme warned as she twisted around to see him.

To his relief, her expression wasn't outraged but puzzled.

"I have always wanted to do that," he confessed with a laugh.

She raised one brow haughtily. "I assume you mean

during our arguments—or was it every time you laid eyes on me?"

He waggled his eyebrows, and traced the faint outline of his fingers on her white skin. "Usually as you walk away from me. I've often wanted to reach out, throw you over my knee, and spank you for making such devastating use of the naughty tongue in your head. You've the devil in you some days, I swear."

Esme flattened herself on the bed, resting her head on her folded arms. "I'm rather restrained compared to some."

"Believe me, you are certainly not." Richard bent and kissed the mark he'd made because his heart truly wasn't interested in punishing her. He just wanted to do everything with her, at least once, to see how she'd react. He was going to store up her every reaction for later use. He intended to have ample material at his disposal when he met with her during the coming months. It was about time he had something to hold over her head.

"You are exciting." He ran his fingers along her sides. "Do you enjoy lovers who spank you?"

"Occasionally."

He pressed a kiss to her waist and whispered, "What other naughty things do you like to do, Esme?"

"Richard, you don't need any suggestions to improve your technique with me."

He grinned at her rare use of his given name. So far she'd only said it, screamed it, during release. He took in her form—arms raised; bare, tempting skin—and rejoiced in his good fortune in being her lover at last. He'd never intended to become intimately involved with Esme but he couldn't imagine denying himself the satisfaction of making love to her.

He slid his fingers around her ankles and widened her legs, posing her so he could glimpse the damp pink lips of her quim.

But if she were standing, she would be the most perfect

Hill bride in history.

He swallowed hard at that train of thought. Damn Oswin for suggesting it. He could actually imagine abducting, tethering and fucking Esme in the dark forest according to family tradition. Where he normally grew appalled at the notion, imagining Esme that way filled him with intense desire to take her there tonight. Gods he wanted her. Wanted to keep her. Wanted to fuck her all night and every night for the rest of his life.

He hung his head and tried to push the desire away. He couldn't do that to Esme; take her to the woods, not without her permission or at least feeling she could accept such a situation.

He turned her over and crawled onto the bed. He set his hands on each side of her shoulders and stared into her eyes. "Have you ever been bound for sex?"

Her smile was amused. "Yes."

"And?"

"It is not something a woman should do without knowing the man very well." She touched his face with just the tips of her fingers. "I like to use my hands."

He quivered as she stroked his throat and then moved on to caress his chest. She teased his nipples, her bottom lip pinched between her teeth. He had to know. "Would you trust me to restrain you, should the opportunity arise during a tryst?"

She slid her hands down his sides. "What do you have in mind, lover?"

He met her gaze hesitantly and saw only amusement reflected in her eyes. "That, I cannot confess. It is a fantasy that I am wary to speak of."

"I would trust you not to hurt me." She smiled then, blindingly bright and honestly. She raised her hands above her head and mimicked being bound for him. "I believe no matter the position, I would always find pleasure with you."

Richard kissed her hard.

All his life he'd been somewhat ashamed of his family's history with women. With the manner in which they took their wives, and the perpetuation of a superstition that promised prosperity and relied on blind faith. It was ridiculous, backward, and utterly wrong in this day of enlightenment. He'd never intended to take his bride, but he could share a night like that with Esme for all the right reasons. He knew it bone deep that he wanted to have her, make her tremble with pleasure until she screamed.

He would not be using her or degrading her. Esme was beautiful and confident in her nudity. She was everything he wanted in a woman.

Her gaze skimmed down his torso and dropped to his erection. He ached for her to touch him. She did, but softly, the tips of her fingers trailing fire up and down his length. She skimmed the head of his cock with her finger, spreading his seed all around.

When she raised her finger to her lips and licked it clean, he growled. "So be it."

He lowered himself to her body and wrapped her arms and legs about him. They kissed, deeply and with all the skill they possessed. Esme dug her fingers into his hips and urged him to enter her.

"You *do* like me." He filled her, watching her blue eyes widen. "As much as I like you."

"I…" Esme squeezed her eyes shut and drew his head to her shoulder. "Make love to me."

Richard loved her slowly, never allowing the frenzy of their previous couplings to overtake him. The feelings she'd already stirred in him amplified. With her legs wrapped around him, her hands clutching his sides, he felt something shift inside him a little more. He could get used to this feeling. He could get used to her being in his life.

As he drew back to look into her face, Esme shifted to force him up to his knees and rolled to her stomach beneath him. Then she set her arms to the mattress and rose. She presented him with her pert little bottom and Richard reentered her from behind, fighting an urge to grasp her hair and fuck her hard and fast. He'd fought the same inner battle their first night as lovers and almost lost his mind trying to hold back.

Richard liked this position too much. In this pose, Esme was as submissive as he'd likely ever find her. He skimmed a hand along her back, over her shoulder, and then grasped the back of her neck. He squeezed and Esme's body clenched around his cock like a vise. He bit back an oath. Fighting to keep control as he rammed into her.

He released her and caught her hips firmly with both hands. Esme shuddered and gasped, rocking back into him relentlessly. He increased his pace until she was moaning to every thrust. He grinned at her incoherent babble. Clearly, he wasn't the only one who enjoyed vigorous sex in this manner. So far he'd yet to discover anything she didn't like. Their passions matched; if only their tempers could always. He would take whatever he could get tonight and be content.

He exhaled sharply.

But before the house party ended, he would take her to the woods. He didn't think he could live without this. Without her passionate response to guide his.

Bowing to the inevitable, he set a steadier pace and glanced down. His cock slid wetly from Esme's tight sheath and he threw more of his body weight against her.

She braced herself with her arms, her head lowered to the mattress and her soft moan filled his ears. "Yes, Richard. Oh yes."

He slammed into her hard and fast, causing those soft moans to grow to desperate sobs. He gave her everything he had, his heart slamming against his ribs, his skin slicking with sweat. Damn, but he could make love to her all night and never tire of it.

Esme squeezed him suddenly, her body clenching tightly around his length as she came. He cried out a moment later as his own release spilled inside her. He fell over her, and they knelt there on his large bed, gasping for every breath.

Slowly, Esme crumpled to the mattress and Richard followed, sprawling half over her. He moved her damp hair away from her eyes. "You are amazing."

She caught his fingers and brought them to her lips. All of a sudden, she started to laugh against them. The soft, earthy chuckle filled his soul with wonder. Esme was happy, and he'd caused her to be.

"What is it?"

"I imagine I will regret saying this as soon as tomorrow, but," she kissed his fingers, "you're not so bad yourself."

High praise indeed, but… "Wait and tell me in a few days' time if you still mean it."

Chapter Thirteen

"**I** must say, you've impressed me," Harriet whispered to Esme. They sat alone together in a quiet corner of the drawing room after dinner. "It takes a determined woman to tame that rogue of his wandering eye and by all accounts, Windermere has turned aside every invitation to dabble elsewhere during the last few days."

A pleasant hum of anticipation coursed through her body at the thought of how she'd spent her time during this particular house party. Esme was well satisfied with her unexpected fling. She'd had Richard as a lover and there seemed no wavering of his attention or a reduction in pleasure. "I've not tamed him."

Despite the thrill of her affair, Windermere was not a man to keep around for long. She reminded herself that their time together as lovers was almost over.

Esme yet again considered their affair. Unfortunately, it no longer seemed to align to her deepest wishes to end it, even though she must. During those moments after release when Windermere held her in his arms so tightly, one's breath slowing in time with the other's, their hot bodies cooling, her traitorous thoughts strayed to a future that just might feature more of the man holding her.

A future she couldn't ever take up.

A woman of her years and experience shouldn't delude herself that they had a chance just because he was exciting, funny and rather thoughtful, now she'd spent more time alone with him. He did still annoy her at times, but it had become harder and harder to express her dissatisfaction out loud. She didn't want to spoil their time together. It was his knowing smile, perhaps, or the discreet slide of his hand over her body that silenced her and made her think of carnal pleasures so often.

Always, with him.

Harriet pursed her lips a moment then leaned close. "Then you won't mind if he meets with another lady?"

The question jarred Esme. She might have a mutually satisfactory arrangement with Windermere for the time being, but there had never been any doubt she'd lose him to another woman sooner rather than later.

A long-term affair with a man like Windermere was as ludicrous as suggesting she would have a child of her own one day. The earl needed a wife and a son more than a barren lover, no matter how thrilling their intimate encounters were.

A wave of sadness ripped though the idea of Windermere holding his son and shadowy wife in his arms. Caught by surprise, she blinked at the distress such a scene caused her. "No, of course not," she managed to choke out. "He must marry to ensure the succession."

"Oh, Esme. You look about to cry." Harriet gently patted her hand. "Are you certain you could bear it?"

She shook her head to sweep away her confusing feelings. "I must not consider any other outcome. You know what I am."

"Barren," Harriet whispered and then caught up her hand. "I wished it wasn't so, for I've never seen you as content as you have been this week."

"He has faults." However, there wasn't much wrong with him aside from his high opinion of himself. *That* hadn't changed with increased intimacy. He was always fishing for compliments.

"Would it surprise you to learn that Hammond has invited me to visit with him next? I believe I will take him up on his generous offer and go there after the party, instead of returning to London."

Esme snapped her attention back to her friend. "I thought you were eager to go home to your son?"

"Alexander doesn't really need me." Harriet sighed. "His uncle likely won't want me there either. He writes often to say my son has blossomed under his care."

Harriet had a difficult relationship with her son and her late husband's family. Her son listened too much to them and disregarded his mother at every opportunity.

"A change of scenery would be nice and Hammond has been going on about his new property so much that I'd like to see the place for myself." Harriet's gaze darted across the room and a frown creased her brow. "Yes, a new view of a different countryside will be just the thing for me."

Esme discreetly turned to see what Harriet peeked at.

Lord Avery Hill had rejoined the party at last. He'd not been seen for several days and Esme had assumed he'd left the estate entirely. Dressed to perfection, the gentleman appeared no worse for wear and was even bowing over the hand of a lady he'd insulted while deep in his cups. Judging by the lady's smile, all had been forgiven between them. "He appears to have recovered his composure."

Harriet lifted her fan and beat it furiously before her face. "He indulged in a fit of childish pique at being refused, nothing deeper."

Esme did not believe that for a moment. "He did seem genuinely upset when we spoke."

Her friend snapped her fan shut. "If he was indeed as distraught as you claim, might the man not have taken steps to keep me in his life? I've seen nothing of him for days and now he's flirting with every woman who comes near him."

As Lord Avery buckled over and laughed heartily at a jest made by another smiling lady, Esme groaned. Perhaps she had been wrong about him after all. "I see your point."

"Now whose point are we discussing? Mine, I hope." Miles Hammond dropped into the space at Harriet's left and caught up her hand. When he kissed the back of it, Harriet blushed and fluttered her fan before her face. The two of them shared a secret smile.

Esme gaped at them. "What are you doing?"

"I rather think that is obvious." Hammond smiled wickedly. "Are you feeling left out of my affections, sweetheart? There's always room for you in my heart."

His sudden switch from friend to the appearance of a hungry swain set her teeth on edge. "Don't be absurd."

Hammond shrugged. "Suit yourself."

He leaned close to Harriet and whispered in her ear. Whatever confidence he shared caused Harriet to laugh softly and lift her hand to his face. "What a delicious idea."

Esme tore her gaze away from the flirting couple, utterly shocked to her core. Harriet and Hammond? Not in a million years could they be right for each other beyond friendship.

Lord Avery Hill hadn't missed the romantic exchange between Harriet and Hammond either. His smile slipped away as he openly stared at the couple. He clenched his fists at his side and Esme closed her eyes. This was worse than attending the theatre.

Hammond chuckled again, pressed a kiss to Harriet's fingers. "Until later, sweetheart."

When he excused himself, Esme pounced on Harriet for an explanation immediately. "What do you think you are doing with him?"

"I am living the life I want to live," Harriet declared

hotly.

"Are you sure?" Harriet had wanted a life with Lord Avery Hill. She'd confessed herself in love with the scoundrel. And Harriet never fell hard for anyone. "This new direction into Hammond's arms makes not the smallest amount of sense. You've always been wary of his dark nature. You don't like what he likes."

"Our interest in each other is very real, I assure you." Harriet smiled tightly. "Do not interfere."

"I don't mean to interfere but I do question your judgment. Hammond couldn't be more wrong for you," Esme warned. "I'm afraid you're making a terrible mistake without thinking of the consequences."

"He wants to change. To settle down, and in that our interests align." Harriet held her ground a moment longer then her shoulders sagged. "Must you always have to stick your nose where it's not wanted?"

"I thought I knew what you wanted, so of course I will speak up." She frowned severely. "You don't have the same tender feelings for Hammond as you have for another man who shall remain nameless. You're playing with fire and I don't like to see either of you hurting yourselves when there's no reason to. You're my friends."

Harriet shrugged. "We are not playing, Esme."

"Oh!" she stuttered, and took another quick glance around the room. "Well, a certain idiot is openly staring at you, so I'm not the only one surprised by your changed relationship with Hammond."

"Kettle. Pot. Black." Harriet tossed her head. "Windermere stares at you just as much tonight. Wasn't there a part of you that wanted revenge against Meriwether when he announced his marriage?"

She had indeed. She sank into the chair, feeling embarrassed with her outburst. She had no call to question the way Harriet lived her life when her own love life was just as unconventional.

"I suppose you are right. I'm sorry, my friend. I'm just as guilty of playing with fire as you are." She met Harriet's gaze and her friend nodded, accepting her apology. "He does that a lot. Stares at me, I mean."

But when she glanced across the room to where Richard stood in mixed company, her pulse jumped in the most disconcerting way because he *wasn't* paying her any attention.

Look at me, lover.

Richard turned his head in her direction and heat smoldered in his blue eyes when their gazes met.

The corner of his mouth lifted in a subtle smile of acknowledgement.

"Well, you are exquisite." Harriet laughed softly. "We both deserve to be noticed."

She lowered her eyes quickly, disconcerted by how much she craved Windermere even now. They had met briefly this morning in his study, a fast and furious tongue lashing across his mahogany desk that had sent papers and ornaments crashing to the floor. Heat warmed her cheeks and she could almost feel his breath beating across her skin as he whispered her name in the wake of her release. A release he'd not shared this time. It was the first time he'd ever held back. She owed him and would repay him soon, but she had to get her traitorous libido under control first.

"Ladies." Richard's deep voice interrupted her train of thought, sending tremors of lust tumbling through her limbs. "I trust you have everything you need."

Her pussy quivered as she met his gaze. *Not yet.*

"Oh, yes." Harriet glanced between them and then chuckled softly. "But I was telling my dear friend how weary I am this evening. I was about to wish her a good night and retire. Until tomorrow."

Esme watched her friend saunter out then braced herself. She was not so undone by her desires to let a man, and everyone else in the room, see she was as close to being out of control as it was possible to be.

"Penny for your thoughts," he said softly as he took Harriet's place at her side.

Her thoughts were filled with his gasps and moans and the intensity of his lovemaking. She swallowed down her panic. She did not want to need Richard like this. They had no future together, but as soon as she saw him her thoughts quickly plotted out how to drag him off to a quiet room and make mad, passionate love. "I was thinking of this morning."

"What a wonderful coincidence. So was I." He studied the clock over the mantelpiece, the tip of his tongue resting on his upper lip momentarily. "Care for another?"

Her pussy clenched in memory of what that tongue could make her feel. "I do owe you for this morning."

"I thought to wait until tonight." The corners of his mouth lifted into a wicked smile as he held her gaze. "I would be so happy if you could indulge me particularly tonight in something a little unusual."

Esme nodded eagerly, though a little frightened by how her feelings had changed for him. A week ago she would have laughed at the idea that she looked forward to being intimate with Windermere. Now, she couldn't wait to strip him of every piece of clothing he possessed. Even a few minutes' wait suddenly seemed an eternity until he touched her. Esme slipped her hand over his thigh and squeezed. "Yes."

"Thank you." He stared at where her hand rested and she jerked it back, astonished by what she'd done in public. They did not ordinarily touch where anyone could see such caresses. Esme preferred discretion in her lovers. In herself too. A hand held to exit a carriage or to dance was far different from groping his thigh in front of his guests. Heated glances were normally the only outward display of emotion she allowed herself in public.

"I think we should slip away sooner than later." He met

her gaze and exhaled slowly. "Meet me outside my study on the terrace in five minutes. There are a few things we will need."

"Anything you wish."

"I was hoping you'd say that." When he excused himself after a long interval of silence, Esme was glad to see him go. She was embarrassed, and she hadn't felt this unbalanced for a long time. Had she ever felt this way for a lover?

Esme slowed her breathing deliberately in an attempt to regain control. She had a few minutes to wait and then she could escape into his arms. She frowned. Since when had she ever fallen apart when a man so much as suggested a tryst? She did not need men in her life. She chose to have them for the fun of it. Making love to Richard was exciting but all too addictive. To her chagrin, they were as well-matched out of bed as in it, of late.

There hadn't been anything to disagree about since their first night together, actually.

As the clock reached the appointed moment, Esme all but flew out of her seat, hurried along to his study, and let herself into the poorly lit room. Richard stood in the open doorway, lantern and burlap sack stacked at his feet. He picked up a cloak—her own, she discovered—and dressed her in it. "The woods can be cold. I hope you don't mind riding at night."

"No, of course not," she whispered, picking up on the tension in his voice.

He took her hand in his and before she could draw back, he bound her wrists together firmly. She tested her bonds. "I see the reason behind your questions now."

He led her toward the stables by the dangling end of rope without a word and when they reached the dark structure, the unlikely figure of Oswin holding two saddled horses appeared from the shadows.

The butler bowed formally. "Good evening, my lady."

If the butler thought it odd she was bound and being led around, he said and did nothing to suggest it. "Oswin."

Oswin held the bridle of her mare as Windermere lifted her into the sidesaddle and made sure she was secure in her stirrups. He gave her the reins to hold, and then mounted his own horse, settling his sack on his lap before he took her horse's bridle from Oswin.

The butler backed away, taking the lantern with him.

"I'll lead you," Richard insisted.

Esme sighed. "I can ride on my own, even with my hands bound like this."

"Would you rather be put over my lap on the saddle?"

She gaped. "Windermere, what's got into you?"

"You…and there's only one thing left to do about you." He shook his head. "No more talking until we're away from the house."

Chapter Fourteen

Richard rode directly into the woodland enclosure and dismounted his horse, running through the litany for the night ahead. He could still feel the touch of Esme's hand on his thigh from the drawing room. He was ready for her, so hard that riding had been a painful experience he never wanted to repeat.

He turned his attention to the woman he'd abducted. So far, she'd barely complained about his silence and treatment. He expected her to have a lot to say soon when he threw her over his shoulder for the climb up the mount.

She didn't appear to like being helpless.

Neither did he like to make her so, but if he was going to do this, he had to do it all more or less properly.

He approached her, grasped her about the waist and deposited her outside the gate of the enclosure with perfunctory care. The histories expected him to bend his bride to his will. He wanted to kiss Esme witless instead.

He tended their horses with brisk efficiency and then faced her. Esme, however, had wandered away, staring up at the dark canopy overhead, her demeanor calm and unruffled by his behavior. Richard gritted his teeth for the next part and pursued her. He hoisted her over his shoulder before she realized his intent. Her shriek of shock echoed in the night. "Fight me all you want but it must be this way."

He grappled with the sack while she struggled to regain her freedom.

"This is ridiculous," she complained.

He was not supposed to react to pleas for mercy. He was supposed to be a bloody tyrant about this abduction and force her to go with him by any means.

He gritted his teeth against softening. He'd decided to give the family tradition this one chance to be proven false. He might never get another chance for months, so it was tonight or never.

He made the trek uphill as best he could, her complaints ringing in his ears and turning them pink. At the point where she'd begun repeating herself, he'd already reached the high lookout, a break in the woodland that afforded the best views for miles around. The place was lit by moonlight almost as clearly as it would be on a summer's morning.

Three large stones had been placed around the base of a tree that had once thrived, although now resembled a weathered stump. Roughly six feet from the base, an iron spike had been hammered into the wood.

And that was where he took Esme and secured her so she couldn't get away.

She blew out a breath, moving her fallen hair from her eyes. "I could have walked," she told him, her tone full of sarcasm.

He couldn't have her too angry, so he gently smoothed her hair back from her face until it was neat. "Then where would be the fun in seeing me sweat?"

Her gaze raked him. "Why are you doing this?"

"Because I want to and because I must." He kissed her, cupping her face and devoured the mouth that had just flayed his manhood, his honor, his character on the long walk up the mountainside.

He stood back eventually, leaving her panting and still bound. Her breasts rose and fell rapidly and he bared them to the evening air, grateful for the front fastenings on her gown. Her nipples hardened as the cooler air hit them and he played with one. "You are so beautiful. Everything I've ever wanted in a woman."

A soft gasp left her lips as he tugged harder.

"Even when you're angry with me, I can still affect you." He bent his head and licked her nipple before taking the tip into his mouth and sucking for a while.

Esme whimpered when he eased back and he blew over the tip lightly, torturing her. He could do that as long as she enjoyed it. She thrashed against her restraints, no doubt seeking to escape her bonds to hold his head to her breast, the way she'd shown him she preferred in the past days.

He turned away to rummage through the sack instead. A bottle of brandy, a fine glass wrapped in silk, a phallus made in the image of his manhood, and a soft wool blanket to wrap her in afterward.

Next, he stripped. He removed everything he wore and laid it aside in a neat pile, everything except the ring bearing the family crest that always graced his left hand.

He poured the brandy and took the glass to her. "Drink."

To his surprise, she obeyed, her expression full of questions. He refilled the glass and turned it so he'd place his lips exactly where hers had been. He downed the lot quickly, hating the taste. However, the ritual demanded this particular elixir as the accompaniment.

Not for the first time did he wonder if his ancestors had drugged all their brides and themselves to get through this night.

He wouldn't do that to Esme. One glass for each of them would have to be sufficient.

He put the glass aside, and lifted his cravat from his pile of clothes. He ran the fabric through his hands and then tied the stark white linen around her tiny waist. He stood back and then paced the circle, first clockwise then turned back time by walking in another direction.

He felt utterly ridiculous.

When he was directly behind her back, he danced a few stumbling steps of a country dance.

"Richard," Esme called, her tone full of exasperation. "Come back and kiss me."

He rushed to her, eager to answer her summons. Richard pressed his hips against hers. "My darling Esme."

He kissed her, dragged her gown up her slim legs so they were skin to skin from the waist down. Despite being bound and essentially his prisoner, Esme made her desire abundantly clear in the way she pressed her body to his.

He caught one of her thighs and she jumped to wrap her legs about his waist, arms still secured above her head. She flexed her body so her quim rubbed against his hard cock. He caught her legs and shifted each so her feet rested on rocks placed to either side of the stump. Positioned in this manner she was entirely open to him, entirely helpless.

She braced herself against the tree trunk and took in what he'd done. Her gown rested on the top of her thighs and he nudged it higher still, baring her quim.

"Oh, my word," she whispered. "Am I your slave tonight?"

He closed his eyes, feeling horrible and helpless, but unable to stop now he'd begun. He'd never expected to be as aroused by Esme like this as he was. He was desperate for her. "You belong to me."

Without the barrier of clothing or position in his path, he slid into her body effortlessly. A few thrusts and he was properly seated. Esme moaned darkly and sought his mouth for a kiss.

In this, Esme's satisfaction was supposed to come

second, but he kissed and touched her, aroused her, and did all he could to make her respond as he claimed her.

Beneath his grunts, Esme sighed and moaned, unwittingly encouraging him to continue. He held her face, fingers framing her jaw and holding her steady. Met her gaze as he ground into her. She came apart, shrieking his name like the wildest of woodland creatures.

She sagged in her bonds, helpless but sated. "This was your fantasy all along. To have your way with me like this. That's why you asked what I'd allow."

He slowed his thrusts. "It hadn't been at first, but…"

"I do trust you. I want you to come inside me like this," she whispered. "I want you to have your darkest desires come true with me."

His body flooded with heat at her words. His desire to keep Esme in his life became a desperate, palpable need. He wanted to marry her. He pledged his heart and his soul to her keeping, and with his body, begged her own in return. He fucked her harder than ever and when he exploded so powerfully, he almost couldn't breathe for the thrill of it.

He told her the truth then. A truth he hadn't realized until that moment he was so urgent to share.

"I love you, Esme. I couldn't ever want anyone the way I want you. Not like this. You're mine and I'm yours. Completely and forever."

Chapter Fifteen

Esme quickly shook off the happiness Richard's declaration of love evoked. No man meant such a declaration so soon after climax, and she knew that all too well. However, her heart wasn't listening to her head at the moment and rejoiced instead that Richard felt so much for her as to want to say such sweet and tender things.

She flexed her fingers above her head where they were still tied. Her arms were beginning to ache from the position. The dead tree she was tied to was not at all comfortable either for her back. She hoped Richard's fantasy, at least the part involving tying her up, was done with for tonight and he'd soon cut her down. She wanted to touch him so much.

When she'd taken a moment to really look at and listen to Richard when they'd first arrived at the clearing, she'd understood he'd been very nervous about sharing so intimate a fantasy.

It did seem a little out of character for him, but she hadn't truly minded being bound. Restrained as if she were a barbarian's conquest—stolen in the night as if she had no choice. She'd had a choice, and had chosen Richard. She did trust him and his fevered lovemaking had given her great pleasure in return.

As he withdrew, she exhaled and placed her feet back on the ground. "Ah, that's better."

He unhooked her hands and before she could take even one step, he lifted her into his arms and held her against his heaving chest as if he was still her master. "Did I hurt you?"

"Of course not. I would have certainly mentioned any real discomfort." He laid her out on a large rock that was still warm from the sun and lifted her skirts again. He untied the cravat around her waist and set it aside. She pushed at him, eager to be free to run her hands over his body too. "Let me up."

"I'm not done yet," he warned.

"Truly?" She frowned at him but reclined again. His cock was soft and he did not appear even a little amorous. "What else do you want to share with me?"

He held up a dildo and kissed the tip. "This."

He spread her legs and gently invaded her with it. After so much pleasure from his cock, she shrunk away from the chilled intrusion. "That's cold."

"Forgive me." Next he bound her legs together at her knees with his cravat and pulled her skirt over her legs. He flung the blanket over her and stood back. "That's it."

"Richard, I cannot walk like this."

"You're not supposed to walk anywhere just yet." He bit his lip. "We have to stay here a while longer."

She frowned at that. "But we *are* going back to the manor tonight," she told him.

"Yes, soon."

He left her there, hands bound, knees strapped together, an uncomfortable feeling growing inside her. This was not the man she'd come to know. Richard Hill, Earl of Windermere, was a gentleman to the tips of his perfectly polished hessians. A lion in the bedchamber, but not so perverse as to leave a woman in discomfort.

Or so she had thought.

He returned half dressed and watched her silently as he buttoned himself up in his clothing. There was a peace about him she'd not seen ever before. He appeared confident. Content. Pleased, when she was so helpless.

She licked her lips to wet them. "How long have you wanted to bring a woman here?"

"Not long," he murmured, toying with a lock of her hair that spread out toward him. He sifted the strands between his fingers then carefully returned it to the rock she lay upon.

"Why tonight?"

He glanced up at the sky. "The moon is full and the house party is a success. I was confident everyone would be too busy to wonder where we had gone. It was the right time."

"Oswin knows."

"And knows enough to keep his mouth shut about what we're doing here," he insisted.

She glanced around them as fear crept into her thoughts. She twisted a little to take in her surroundings again. It was very strange to have a dildo inside her body without using it for pleasure, and they were very alone. "Will I be murdered next?"

"That is what I thought you'd ask." He chuckled softly then stroked her cheek with the backs of his fingers. "I'd never hurt you. I wouldn't dare, and I don't want to except for the occasional spanking you might require."

That wasn't reassuring. She lifted her head and struggled. "I want to leave."

"As you wish." He sighed and flung the blanket away, unbound her knees and then carefully removed the dildo. He flung it away, into the woods lying dark below them. "Is that better?"

"Yes." She eased off the rock and put a little distance between them, quickly buttoning the front of her gown so she was decent again. Her hair she couldn't do much about but it was undoubtedly tangled.

"Oh, you should see your face." He laughed outright then, like a young man in love with his life and everything in it. "Come, come, Esme. Let us walk back to the horses arm in arm as the very good friends we are. I have what I want."

"What is it you wanted?"

His laughter died. "Everything. To make love to you in the most significant way a man in my family could. Without doubt or holding back anything I was feeling."

When he stretched out his hand, she accepted it. Assured he wasn't about to murder her, she drew close to him. He tucked her arm through his and led her toward the path he'd traversed carrying her over his shoulder. She'd been too wrapped up in scolding him to notice the terrain wasn't smooth or even. Far fewer people went to the mount than must go to the woodland glade. She shivered, understanding the effort the trek must have required and impressed he'd carried her up the mount in the first place to save her the hardship.

He tugged her along until they reached the horses then helped her mount. He was gentle and sweet and not at all like the man who'd thrown her over his shoulder and carried her off like a barbarian intent on ravishing her.

She'd enjoyed his ravishment, actually.

They rode in silence again but she couldn't stop looking at him. He *was* different somehow.

His smile widened suddenly and she grew alarmed. "Why are you smiling like that?"

"It seems Oswin couldn't keep his mouth shut after all." He pointed ahead. Lanterns had been placed at regular intervals from the stables leading toward the manor house. "You're being directed home, my lady."

"Home?"

He nodded. "In my family, every woman a Hill takes

into the woods, to the high clearing, becomes a bride that morning. It's tradition to take the woman you want to marry to the wishing tree to ask for the blessing of offspring and prosperity."

Her stomach dropped. "I'm not a bride. You are certainly not my husband."

"Not in a legal sense, no." He smiled without concern for her protest. "Not yet."

"Not ever." She reined in her mount. "I will not marry you."

"You already did. I gave you my heart, my soul, in those woods. I am in love with you, and that only happens once for a Hill."

"You did not mean it," she protested. "No man or woman ever means what is said during intimacy. You cannot love me."

"I do. I will always love you."

She peered ahead and noticed shapes moving in the shadows. "Dear God, there's a welcoming party?"

"You were a popular choice. My butler even pulled me aside and demanded to know what my intentions were. I didn't have any that day, but I do now."

Esme covered her face. "Stop this nonsense, Richard. I cannot and will not marry you."

"Why wouldn't you?"

She kicked her feet clear of the stirrup and dismounted recklessly without help. She staggered away from the horses, horrified that he'd not understood. Darkness was better than facing up to an impossible situation.

Richard must have dismounted too because he grabbed her and tried to embrace her. "You love me. I know you must."

"Love doesn't matter."

"It matters to me."

Esme pushed hard against him, seeking solitude. "Love won't matter one bit when I deny you the son you need. I told you I was barren. I cannot have children."

"We will in time," he protested. "Esme, I cannot marry someone else and feel this way about you."

"Of course you can, and you must. Your happiness matters a great deal to me, but it will matter even more to the people who look up to you, depend on you. You need a son and I cannot ever give you one. I will not go through a second marriage like that."

"Surely—" he started but when she held up her hand for silence, he held his tongue.

"You and your people deserve better than me. I am, as my husband so succinctly put it once, as barren as a brick. I will never give you a child, much less an heir."

He was silent a moment.

"I know my limitations, Richard. I have never conceived. Not once with the dozen or so lovers I've had since becoming a widow." She held out her arms. "Why do you think my affairs are short-lived? They must be. Too much is riding on your succession for me to be so selfish as to allow this. I will not permit the title to pass to Adrian Hill's offspring if I can help it. You must marry someone else and have a child with them."

"I had hoped you were simply trying to reassure me you had no expectations beyond being my lover." He dragged her into his arms. "I'd thought you put on a brave face so you couldn't be hurt if we fought again."

"The bravest face I possessed to hide my disappointment in *myself*. I told you our first night together that there was no need to worry because it's the painful truth."

"But I need you," he whispered as he kissed her brow. "I couldn't have gone through with the ritual with anyone but you. I've never wanted to do that to any woman."

She stilled. "Ah, so it was not your fantasy but a duty."

"Yes," he hissed. "I like your hands on me too."

"Then you must remember your duty to your family.

Find yourself another woman to wed. I am sure she will easily love you." Her voice caught on the last word and she shook her head as she discovered her claim was all too real. She had fallen in love with him, and now she had even more incentive to give him up than ever. "We had a wonderful dalliance and it must end."

"No. We can be together until I find a bride."

"And risk hurting yourself even more." She evaded his embrace. "Be reasonable."

He took a step in her direction and teased her jaw with the tips of his fingers. "Tell me I didn't imagine how good it was between us?"

She wanted to turn into his embrace for comfort, but it would be a mistake and might make him think there was hope.

"It was good." She smiled that he could still need her reassurance. "You are the best lover I've ever had."

He bit his lip. "So the sex is all that counts with you."

"Telling you I fell in love with you too would change nothing." She stroked her fingers down his face one last time. "Be at peace, Richard, and take my dreams with you. I'll hope they come true for you soon."

"Don't go," he whispered when she eased back.

"I have no choice. I can't stay." She strode toward the house but without intending to encounter any of the Hill family servants who sought to welcome the new *bride* home. Her heart ached as she quickened her steps, almost running away from Richard and all he'd blindly offered. As she went, she wiped away the tears streaming down her cheeks. She'd marry Richard in a heartbeat if only she wouldn't ruin his life in the process.

Desperate for comfort from one who would understand her pain, she made her way to Harriet's bedchamber and knocked on the heavy door. "It's Esme."

The door opened quickly and instead of Harriet, she faced Miles Hammond in a state of undress. She forced her emotions away, along with her shock at seeing him there after midnight.

He blinked. "Sweetheart?"

"I need Harriet," she whispered.

He ushered her inside and closed the door behind them.

Harriet was sitting up in bed in a demure nightgown. She spared Esme a fleeting glance and then grimaced. "Windermere took *you* to that damn wishing tree too, didn't he? Perverse bastard."

Harriet threw herself out of bed and rushed to embrace her.

"He's not like Avery," Esme promised. She winced at the broken quality of her voice and straightened her spine. "He imagines us married."

Harriet spat out a bark of bitter laughter. "Marriage? That's new. They never talk about it openly but it's actually a fertility ritual dating back hundreds of years, and particular to this locality." Harriet urged her toward a chair and wiped her tears away with the cuff of her sleeve. "Carolyn Hill explained the significance to me recently. Avery uses it for his own twisted purpose, but I had thought Windermere was above such nonsense."

"Wasted on me," Esme sobbed. "There's nothing that can make me pregnant. I've long given up on that dream."

"Oh my darling," Harriet whispered as she rocked Esme like a babe in arms. "I am so sorry he's hurt you with this. What can I do?"

Esme sniffed. He'd hurt them both, and there was nothing to be done but make a graceful exit as soon as possible. "Can I go with you both when you leave? I need to get away from this place."

"Of course you can." Hammond agreed, pouring drinks at the sideboard. "We can even leave today; the sun will be up in a few hours. I was thinking another month spent in the country would be just the shot before winter sets in. We can make merry together and forget these blasted Hills ever existed."

"I'd like that," Esme whispered, but feared forgetting Richard might just be impossible. She'd like to try though. "I don't think I can face him or London for a long time."

Hammond handed her a glass. "I'll make you both smile again, I swear it."

Chapter Sixteen

The drawing room chatter was strangely subdued as Richard rejoined his guests for a late breakfast or early luncheon. He'd overslept unfortunately by a wide margin, so this was his first chance to begin his campaign to get back into Esme's good graces. Having her smile warmly in his direction again was a priority.

Getting her to talk about their marriage was next, and her insistence she couldn't give him children. She'd never delivered a child, but for the first time last night, he'd understood how that lack hurt her. What could it hurt to try for a child together? He was certainly interested in bedding her as often as she'd allow to make a good try of it.

He glanced around but couldn't see her at first, so he helped himself to a plate of cakes and chose to mingle with the ladies who'd gathered around Mrs. Hill, offering well-meaning advice on her impending motherhood. As one, they brushed aside his attempts to converse. Even Carolyn wouldn't look at him, and he puzzled over that new development.

Esme would tell him what he'd missed and undoubtedly tell him what to do. He pursed his lips to hide a smile.

God, she never could stop, and he didn't ever want her to.

What he'd found in Esme was the one person who made him happier than he'd ever been—both in bed and out of it. They had always been honest, especially about the things that mattered. If she believed herself barren he'd accept it, but that did not mean they couldn't be together as man and wife.

He took a tour of the room again, noticing by the end that Esme was not present. It was hard to miss that most guests appeared openly hostile toward him and didn't want to talk even while they sipped his best champagne. In desperation for a friendly face, he found Jillian and pulled her aside. "What's going on?"

"Well, nothing beyond the usual. The ladies have had a fine day. We set up our easels in the conservatory and painted each other. Some of the results were amusing."

"Some?" He couldn't wait to see Esme's efforts. She wasn't particularly fond of creating art as far as he could tell, but she never let Jillian down and always encouraged the other women to participate. "Can I look forward to a display?"

"Later today, I think it should be, before the guests start departing tomorrow. Oswin will set everything up in the library. I had considered the long gallery as a venue but perhaps that wouldn't be very kind to force comparisons to the greater painters hung there on us all."

"A wise decision." He bit his lip as Lord Hogan glanced their way. Esme's warning prodded his memory. In the excitement of his budding relationship with her, he'd neglected to pass along her message to his sister, but he could remedy that now, hoping he wasn't about to blunder. "There's something I've been meaning to talk to you about. Might we speak in private?"

Jillian took his arm and he led her farther away to a quiet corner.

He didn't waste any time. "I've been meaning to speak

to you about your future."

"Oh?"

She appeared startled and he rushed on so she didn't get the wrong idea. "I wanted to be sure you knew I am happy to have you home and reassure you there is no reason to rush into another relationship if you'd rather not."

His sister's shoulders relaxed. "For a moment, I wasn't sure you were going to give me your blessing or marching orders."

He glanced toward Hogan again. "The gentleman's not spoken to me. Is it serious between you two?"

She smiled softly. "No. Well, maybe once I entertained a notion, but my eyes are opened now."

Richard folded his arms across his chest. "Esme spoke to you already, didn't she? I told her I would do it. That woman will be the death of me."

"Not soon enough, brother dear." Jillian smiled a touch sadly. "But yes, Esme spoke to me several days ago. Said I should make up my own mind and I have taken my time forming my own opinions during the house party."

Curiosity burned when she didn't elaborate immediately. "And?"

"She was right about Lord Hogan." Jillian fidgeted. "There is nothing he likes more than an idea he put forward himself and to subtly ridicule others so I might think less of them. He hasn't a kind word to say about Esme and suggested we shouldn't even be friends already, if you can imagine. She warned me he'd try to subvert my friendships first, and she was right."

Richard's hackles rose. "You keep your friendship with Esme, with anyone you choose."

"I will." Jillian shrugged. "I just hope recent events will not prevent her from being friends with me. I do like her more than any other female acquaintances you've had."

He shuffled his feet. He shouldn't have delayed seeking out Esme a moment longer than necessary. "I cannot imagine Esme would ever snub you."

"She might." Jillian stared at him, eyes narrowing. "Did you have to be such a scoundrel with no thought to her feelings?"

Richard glanced around quickly, realizing everyone must know they'd argued last night. How they could know he wasn't sure but he would fix everything soon. "You know how hot her temper can be. It's just a misunderstanding. By tomorrow all will be settled between us."

"That would be difficult."

"Esme can be entirely sensible when she wants to be. I can be very persuasive."

Jillian gripped his arm and stared into his face until he grew uncomfortable. "How did I get so unlucky in my brothers? You are both so entirely witless it breaks my heart. Someone should have told you by now."

"Don't ever lump me in with Avery's follies." Richard scowled. "If he'd just settle on one woman, he wouldn't be so bloody miserable. I'll talk Esme round, never fear."

Jillian shook her head. "Since I've just come from having the same conversation with Avery, I guess I'll have to be as blunt with you too."

He glanced around the room quickly. "Do spit it out. I need to speak with her."

Jillian scowled. "She left this morning in Mr. Hammond's carriage at daybreak, without a word of farewell to anyone but Oswin. The poor man cried, I think."

He searched for one particular face among the far crowd. He swallowed when he didn't find Hammond seated among his guests. "Alone?"

His sister huffed. "Lady Ames and Mr. Hammond went with her. Avery didn't take the news well. I would suggest you don't venture into the morning room until repairs have been made."

He swallowed hard. "She wouldn't have left without

saying goodbye," he insisted. But a hollow feeling filled the pit of his stomach. She had insisted she had to leave last night. He'd not believed her then. He'd certainly not imagined she'd leave without speaking to him again.

Richard noticed again all the disappointed looks aimed his way. "That explains my reception this afternoon."

He took a drink from a servant and sipped, trying to accept he'd already lost Esme.

"Everyone—and I mean everyone but Avery and Lord Hogan—liked Esme for you. I have heard more whispers about the two of you making a match than I have of anyone this Season. Why did you have to follow family tradition and ruin everything by taking her out into the woods?"

"She wasn't upset about the abduction," he told her. "But what it signified for our relationship alarmed her."

"It is customary in our society to allow a woman beyond their first season the luxury of some choice in whom they wed, rather than forcing it on her."

"It wasn't my presumption exactly that upset her." It was worse. She couldn't give him a son and denied them both any happiness. Without a child, she believed there was no reason to wed him.

"Doubly a fool." With that, Jillian rushed off, leaving Richard uncertain of what to do next. He dropped the glass to a nearby table.

A footman with a tray of drinks stared, eyeing him warily from a distance. Richard waved him over. Now that was what he really needed while he formulated a plan to get her back. No doubt she was miles away by now so he had better come up with a compelling reason why the succession wasn't important before he followed.

There was no point rushing Esme to change her mind anyway. He'd never win her over that way. She believed they had no future and only time would prove his devotion sincere. "Another whiskey, Pip. Better make it a dozen. I have some scheming to do."

The footman came close, but then simply shoved the tray toward him. "Have the lot."

Too stunned for words by the servant's surly attitude, he caught the tray before the footman stalked off.

Tucked between the glasses was a folded sheet of paper. He flicked it open one-handed and read.

The paper contained six names, all women. The note was signed with an E and contained a postscript: *don't argue with me.*

He grimaced at her obvious intent—marry one of them, but not her.

"Damn that stubborn woman!" He crumpled the note and rubbed his eye with the heel of his hand. Even when she wasn't here she drove him crazy. How could he choose anyone else after Esme had made him love her?

He'd have to prove her wrong about those other women first and then he'd claim his proper bride at last.

Chapter Seventeen

—◆—

Three months later...

Esme's knees would have given out had she been standing instead of lying flat on her back while a doctor examined her nether regions. Her hands began to shake and she clutched the sheet beneath her tightly to hide her reaction. "I cannot be," she whispered.

Her doctor, a stranger Mr. Hammond had brought to see her against her better judgment, regarded her over his spectacles as he sank into the chair beside her bed, where she'd rested for the last few weeks since her sickness had begun. "Assuredly, you are."

Her head spun, her stomach churned anew. Where was her own doctor when she needed him most, to tell her the real truth? Swooning was definitely a possibility and if she'd been standing, she might forgive herself for indulging in such theatrics given the news that had just been delivered to her. "How can I have a child?"

The man gave her an odd look. "The usual way, I imagine."

Her old doctor in London had explained long ago that she'd likely never conceive a child, no matter how many times Heathcote joined her in bed. She had accepted she would never be a mother and gotten over the disappointment as best she could. Her husband had gotten himself a mistress who had then popped out illegitimate babies at an embarrassing rate, proving Esme the one at fault all along.

Even after her husband had died, Esme had never so much as worried her lovers could get a child on her. None ever had. *Until now.*

She pressed her fingers to her temple as her head throbbed with renewed vigor. "Surely there is room for doubt."

"Of course, but I still expect you to deliver around Easter." He peered at her closely. "Ah, I guess you hadn't hoped for this blessing, after all?"

Hope had been a thing of the very distant past. She'd never dared allow it. "I thought I had simply eaten bad food. I've had the entire kitchen scrubbed out twice just to be sure."

"Well, I am sure your servants will be happy they were blameless in your condition." He smiled warmly. "Try not to panic, my dear. There is no reason you cannot deliver a healthy first child at your age."

"My age?" She rubbed her temple again, fearing her skull would crack from the pounding there. Esme routinely lied about her age. She was a few years older than the doctor knew but she could see no reason to correct him. "That had not even occurred to me as a complication."

"Many women past the first flush of youth go on to deliver safely. Four and thirty is a bit old for a first child, so I would suggest plenty of rest, good food, and a degree of company to distract you from any melancholy that might arise. Surely your husband will understand your fears. You must talk to him, or if you feel yourself unequal to the task,

I could speak to him personally perhaps before I go."

"Mr. Hammond is not my husband." She raised her gaze to the doctor's, heart sinking at her worsening predicament. "I am a widow."

His eyes narrowed on her cherry-red dressing robe, and his frown grew even more pronounced. He glanced toward the door. She had been staying here as Mr. Hammond's guest at his new estate for the past three months, and no doubt many assumed them related or involved in some fashion. Had Hammond suggested they were close? She wasn't sure, but the doctor was clearly suspicious of their relationship.

He cleared his throat. "I am very sorry to hear it. Surely you have someone in your life to give you the support you need during your confinement."

She sat up and forced her legs to firm so she could stand. She felt as weak as a newborn kitten that had been spun in circles by a terrifying child. "I do thank you for your time."

The doctor caught up his little bag and swept from the room. Esme sank onto the bed again and closed her eyes, still unable to believe she'd be a mother at long last.

Hammond and the doctor conversed in low tones then all was silent save for Hammond's heavy footfalls returning to her bedside. She snapped her eyes open and struggled for composure.

He stopped at the nearby chair and gripped the back with both hands. "What did the good doctor say?"

"Rest and bland food can help." She glanced at his pale face and saw true concern. For all his wickedness, Hammond was a good man. He deserved the truth, but Esme couldn't force the words out.

"Nothing more? No hint of why you're retching?"

Pregnant. Esme swallowed the panic again. She had to think and she couldn't do that with Hammond hovering over her. Her friend would never understand how utterly shocked she was feeling at that moment. If only Harriet were here, and not gone off with her son. Esme hadn't the faintest idea what to do. She was not prepared for something like this. "Some, but I don't believe him."

Hammond sat beside her as Esme took a few steadying breaths. But there was no getting over the shock of the doctor's suggestion. Dear God, how could she be pregnant at her age? She'd been so afraid she'd been about to die, casting up her accounts morning and night, never able to keep much at all in her stomach. She'd given up dreams of a child so long ago that she was afraid for even a moment to consider the possibility was real. "Esme, what did he say to you?"

"A young doctor *could* be wrong."

"Perhaps." Hammond slipped his arm behind her back. "Tell me what he said that he could be wrong about?"

"He said..." Dear God, how hard it was to confess to something she'd given up hope for? She tried again. "He suggested I might, well, it seems as if I am to have a..." Her throat closed and tears filled her eyes. How did women normally describe it? "This is difficult."

Hammond waited patiently without speaking.

"It seems I am with child." Inexplicable joy filled her as soon as the words passed her lips. In a few months, she would hold her son or daughter in her arms. The dream of her youth would become a reality.

"I see," Hammond said slowly. His expression clouded over with remorse. "When are you going to do something about it?"

Richard's face flashed before her eyes. Not the smug, arrogant mask he liked to slip over his features as he moved about society, but the one she'd come to know from hours spent in his arms. The wickedly confident man she'd come to love despite her misgivings, who still featured in her thoughts night and day. Particularly their nights—and the last one they'd spent together in the woods.

She dreaded telling him because she'd been so utterly confident she couldn't give him what he needed most. A son. "I don't know."

"Can you find what you need here?"

Esme jerked around to stare at Hammond, finally understanding the question he was truly asking of her. He was not speaking of her telling the father of her child, but something much more dangerous. "I will not take such a drastic action as to end this, no matter how sick I have become."

He exhaled loudly but then leaned close to kiss her temple. "Thank God for that. For a moment there I assumed you would take the path many widows take given your circumstances."

She knew of women who drank boiled pennyroyal to abort a pregnancy because their situations did not allow them to keep a lover's child. But that was not without considerable risk to their lives. She wouldn't do it, not to herself and not to Richard. However, a woman of her position would face social ruin to be pregnant out of wedlock. She would be shunned. Held up for ridicule. If Richard didn't marry her, if he couldn't because he'd already committed himself to another, their child would be denied its birthright, excluded from the society it should have belonged too.

Nausea assailed her again and she pressed a scented handkerchief to her mouth. "I would never do that," she whispered against the soft muslin cloth.

"Shall I have the house closed up?"

"No." She glanced at Hammond. "Why would you suggest it?"

He smiled smugly. "Well, I imagine you do need to confront a certain earl about your condition sooner rather than later."

She shook her head.

"Come now, I know the child is his," Hammond

continued. "Very shoddy of him not to practice restraint, but he will do the proper thing in the end, I've no doubt."

He would but she'd sent him into the arms of other women. She'd demanded he marry someone else. She'd been wrong to deny him. It could already be too late. "Richard will not be pleased with me."

Hammond rocked her and the motion stirred her stomach again. "He should have considered that before he was in your bed."

"He did." A light sweat broke out over her skin as she fought the nausea yet again. "I promised him I couldn't bear a child. I never have before and he believed me. *I* believed me."

"Nonsense. I saw how you were together when you thought no one was looking. It was only a matter of time. I've said it before and I'll say it again, the pair of you are besotted."

"Besotted?" Obsessed was a better description for her state of mind then and now.

"He's been rather wild since his house party I hear. Attending every party, dancing and drinking to excess. Flirting with any woman under thirty."

Her eyes filled with tears. "He did what I told him to do. I told him to find someone else to love."

"He's not himself but he would be a fool to turn you aside and you know it. You are exactly what he needs in a wife and he does need an heir."

"What if," she swallowed as a new terror filled her, "what if there is a child and I lose it? The doctor suggested women of my age sometimes have difficulties." Gingerly, she placed her hand over her belly, still unable to believe the situation she was in.

Hammond squeezed her gently. "Don't borrow trouble before you need to."

"You don't understand." She wanted to explain her terror but Hammond didn't place enough faith in her fears.

"You are correct that he would marry me. He needs an heir. Everyone knows it. But I have never been with child before and I am quite terrified to move. I cannot confess I'm carrying a child only to lose it in the process. I simply couldn't bear it."

"Well, you cannot hide the truth from him forever. Think of your reputation. Think of the child's future. You must be married before the birth."

"I know. I think it best I remain here until I am absolutely sure there is a babe and I am well enough for travel. Look at me." She flung her arms wide and glanced down. Her breasts might be a touch tender, but her stomach beneath her gown was still as flat as ever. There was no outward sign she'd conceived, if her roiling stomach and sharper cheekbones were overlooked. "Do I appear the least bit pregnant? He'll believe I'm trying to trick him like his last lover did."

"Surely not."

"Richard vowed never again to take a woman at her word. We discussed it one night after…" She waved a hand about. "It's preposterous to turn around and suggest he do so with me without evidence. I won't have him doubt me or, worse, laugh at the very suggestion." She could not confess to Richard until she was absolutely certain. She couldn't bear to build up his hopes only to dash them when this, whatever it was, might turn out to be but a mistake.

"You are wrong." Hammond stubbornly shook his head. "No gentleman would ever laugh at any lady should she declare him the father of her child."

"Nevertheless, I will wait until I am certain your doctor knows what he's about." Esme eased back on the bed as yet again a wave of nausea swamped her senses. She was so tired and weary. Casting up her accounts at all hours of the day and night and dreaming of Richard endlessly was utterly draining. She pushed at Hammond's shoulder. "I need to be alone again, but promise me you won't say a word of this to anyone."

"I promise, but what are you going to do? Harriet expects you to return to Town next week."

"I'll write only to her about this." She gagged, and scrambled for the pail beside the bed. When she was without her lunch, she lay down with Hammond's assistance. She was still too ill to travel. She wasn't going anywhere in anything that would rock her about. If anyone were to be disappointed, it would be her alone, so she would stay here for the present.

She pressed her head into the pillows as Hammond gently covered her with the comforter and rang for her maid. "I won't return to Town. I will stay here until it's absolutely necessary to leave."

When she was sure, ready to believe herself, if there really was a need, she would seek out Richard. She didn't look forward to the conversation, especially when it might require her to beg him to marry her just to give the child the protection of his name. That wasn't a good way to start any marriage, but given the alternative future ahead, she just might have no choice in the matter.

Chapter Eighteen

———◆———

Early December…

Prepared for battle, Richard stepped from the carriage and strode up the steps of the home Esme had moved to. It had been five months since she'd slipped away from his estate without saying goodbye. The problem for him was, he'd felt like an arse ever since and he'd missed her terribly. He'd been a fool to concede to her demand that he consider anyone else.

He was married in his mind to Esme. Even his cock seemed to think so, for it hadn't risen even in the slightest except in remembrance of her.

And he was sick of pretending he didn't care about her odd behavior. What the devil was she doing rusticating in the countryside? She belonged in the heart of the *ton* not hiding from it.

News of Esme's avoidance of society hadn't reached him for months after their parting. Society had been abuzz with the speculation of her whereabouts but no one had thought to mention she'd actually truly disappeared, and she had cut off everyone in her life.

In frustration and concern, he'd come up to London again hoping to find her, only to meet with no success. No one knew where she was; no one had spoken to her since his house party. In desperation, he'd barged his way into her London townhouse and forced a fortune on her cagey butler for news of her location, but only after he'd begged and pleaded and sworn he only had Esme's best interests at heart.

Discovering she'd taken over one of Mr. Hammond's houses in the country had relieved him. At least if she was with Hammond she'd be taken care of.

But there was something in the way the butler had delivered the news that concerned him. He'd asked if Esme would be returning to London soon and the answer had been a long time coming. It was no.

He rapped the knocker soundly and shivered in the chill air, while rehearsing what he wanted to say most of all clearly and succinctly. He was here to ask for Esme's hand in bloody marriage again, and she had better accept his offer or there would be hell to pay.

The man at the door was instantly recognizable. The footman who had been in his employ until recently, Pip, took great pains to read the card Richard handed over as if they were strangers, rather than former master and servant. His expression gave little away but given the man's sister was Esme's maid, it meant he was in exactly the right place to find the woman he wanted.

"So this is where you found new employment," he murmured, hoping to soften the man and get inside sooner rather than later.

"Indeed," Pip replied in a tone worthy of Oswin's tutelage.

Pip said nothing more than to bade him wait in the hall while he informed his mistress of Richard's arrival.

While he cooled his heels during the long wait, Richard snooped into the nearby rooms. Knickknacks cluttered every space, and he groaned—Esme's current home was a sleepwalker's nightmare, and he'd been doing a lot of that lately.

"Lady Heathcote will see you now."

He followed the servant through a doorway that had been previously closed and found Esme reclining on a chaise. Dressed in dark-blue velvet, she was bundled up beneath a thick quilt and had so many pillows strew around her body that only her head, shoulders and arms were visible. She looked deliciously warm and good enough to pounce on. He bowed instead. "Esme."

"Lord Windermere."

She did not stand and when he drew closer with the intention of kissing her cheek, he noted the pallor of her skin and the dark circles beneath her eyes. Hammond was not taking care of her after all, and he was suddenly furious. Good thing he'd come prepared to fight long and hard to get her back.

He sat down across from her. "You look beautiful posed like that."

"Thank you." Her eyes softened. They talked of the weather, his journey until she seemed at a loss for words. "Why are you here?"

"Isn't it obvious?" He frowned. "I reached the end of your list and have come to extend you an invitation to return to Windermere. I feel badly about how things ended between us."

Her brow rose. "The purpose of my leaving was to get out of the way."

"You were not in my way. I wanted you to stay, remember, and you turned me down. You sent me off to seduce other women, which I have to say wasn't as pleasant to do when ordered to it as you must have imagined a man could find it." He'd felt lost, uncertain, while they'd been apart. As much as he'd tried it her way, there had been no one on her list who could ever replace Esme in his affections. The time wasted on others had only revealed how utterly wrong she'd been about who would suit him for a wife. "I was surprised to find you'd given up London for this place."

"I was leaving tomorrow."

Richard's pulse sped up at the idea he might have missed her if he'd delayed another day. "Where were you going next? Back to London, or to join Lady Ames, wherever that might be?"

"I'm not sure now," she murmured, in a voice very unlike her usual forthright tones.

She met his gaze warily. To Richard's eye she seemed uncommonly nervous about seeing him again. He smiled warmly. Ill kept or not, it was very good to be with her once more. He had so much to tell her of the past months she'd been away from society. "Jillian parted ways with Lord Hogan after the party and tells me she has no intention of keeping up the acquaintance."

"I am not sorry to hear it." She winced and glanced down at her hands. "I hope she suffered no harm from the association."

"She seems more herself, I think. The way she was before her marriage." Richard tilted his head to catch her eye. "You told me the truth about Hogan and I didn't act fast enough for your taste. I learned what he was about, the truth of his nature, after the party. If not for your words of warning, my sister might be miserable today."

"It is fortunate I knew of Lord Hogan's past. I would not have Jillian hurt for anything." She began to rise then sank down again. Her expression became strained.

"I should remember you are right about most things in the future and save myself the bother of questioning you."

She swallowed. "Do give your sister my best and thank you for coming so far to see me."

Was she dismissing him? No, she bloody well wasn't. He moved across the room and squeezed onto the chaise beside her legs. "There are still things I need to say to you."

Her gaze grew wary. "Such as."

Despite the tone of her words, the practiced phrases came rushing back, but he took a deep breath before repeating them. "Esme, what happened between us at the house party haunts me. I have not stopped thinking of you. I enjoyed our time together very much. I came to specifically ask you to give me another chance."

She winced suddenly and her hand flew to her middle, fingers splaying over her belly.

It took a moment for his brain to register that it was not a pillow she clutched to her stomach.

His eyes widened. There was a bump beneath that quilt. One he couldn't dismiss as a product of his imagination. What the devil was she hiding under there?

He reached for the quilt covering her body and slowly drew it back, despite her efforts to keep herself covered. He struggled to breathe. There was nothing beneath the quilt but Esme—and her belly was large, rounded with the evidence of a significant development. One she'd sworn was not possible.

Esme was with child.

She slipped from the chaise and put distance between them. "A gentleman usually asks a lady for permission before exposing them to the discomfort of a cold room."

"Usually I would."

She licked her lips. "I was about to tell you."

He stood but could only stare at her stomach. Lying down as she had been, smothered by a quilt and hidden beneath many pillows had concealed her condition upon his arrival. But he *had* noted the changes in her face. Standing with sunlight bathing her in a soft glow, however, revealed quite the bump where her babe rested. She was gloriously pregnant. Quite far enough along that...

He swallowed to ease the sudden dryness of his mouth.

She was quite far enough along that *he* could be the

child's father very easily. He sank down on the chaise as shock took the strength from his legs.

Why hadn't Esme written him? She must have known he'd be overjoyed.

He glanced at her face, discovering her calm and composed now despite his shock. He would do the right thing. Surely she knew his character, and his heart, well enough to understand he would marry her immediately if given half the chance. She was what he'd come for after all.

His mind spun with horror that he might never have known if he'd followed through with her choices. If he'd married anyone on her list, their child would have been a born a bastard. That couldn't be allowed to happen.

She exhaled loudly then moved to a sideboard, poured a large amount of spirit into a glass and then thrust it at him. "It does take some getting used to."

Richard drained the whiskey in one gulp. "How?"

Esme laughed, a panicked sound that drove away the shock filling him.

"Sorry," he muttered quickly. "Of course I know how. I meant to say how long before the birth?"

"Some months yet. The doctor believes around Easter."

He glanced at her stomach again and made a quick calculation. He grinned. The child *must* be his. He stood immediately. Once, he'd been completely taken in by a woman who claimed to be carrying his child. Esme had exposed the lie, but he'd been left feeling a fool.

This time, he intended to know without a shadow of a doubt. Besides he was desperate to touch her and end the awkwardness between them.

Richard stretched forth his fingers and touched the bump. Esme's stomach was hard beneath his fingertips, rather than the softness of a pillow that might have been bound about her waist if she wished to pretend to a pregnancy. He breathed a sigh of relief at the resistance and warmth he encountered.

Esme wasn't the type to pretend anything.

She would be a mother at last and he was unbelievably happy to discover it. He spread his fingers over her thick velvet gown, curving them around her belly, fully intending to explore this change in her body thoroughly, lost in wonder of the new life growing inside her.

Esme backed up a few steps. "It's true."

"Come back here. I'm not done with you yet. A very wise woman once told me I had to look beneath the surface." He followed her retreat, aware he was all but chasing her around the room.

"Are you not needed back in London?"

Stubborn, foolish woman. They made quite the pair. "To find this elusive perfect woman you spoke of? Esme, I came here today to again ask you to marry me."

Her eyes widened and her breath caught.

He peered into her face, seeing at last how uncertain she was. "I *was* prepared to wait out the banns, but since there is a child involved, I insist we return to London immediately so I can acquire a special license. We will be married before the week is out and then I'll take you home to Windermere, where you belong, so we can spend Christmas there together. Where you are needed and wanted."

She lifted her hand to her temple. Richard pressed his advantage and draped an arm about her shoulders, drawing her near. "Come now, surely you can see the sense in a match between us. The child will have a father, and my name. You can take over the running of the house from Jillian without any difficulty. You've always stepped in when needed in the past and Jillian is very fond of you. She already loves you as a sister."

She broke away. "Is that enough for you?"

Richard stared at her stiff back in irritation. "How about the reason to wed being I am still completely, irrevocably, in love with you?"

Her head turned the slightest amount. "How could you love me still after I sent you away? I ran from you."

"So you did and I'm sure then you believed it the right thing to do. I did what you demanded of me too. I met with Lady Beauchamp and the whole damned list. Wined, dined and discovered I didn't care one whit more for them at the end than at the beginning of our acquaintances. Why didn't you come back to me?"

Her shoulders tensed and then she rubbed her finger over her lip. "I was afraid to believe I was pregnant for a long time, and then I was more afraid I wouldn't keep it. I've been quite unwell, you see. At all hours. Women lose children every day and I didn't dare travel. I was so afraid that if I left here, I'd ruin this one chance I had."

His heart flipped at the tremor of fear behind her words. "Nothing will go wrong, and if it does, I'll bear the disappointment with you."

Esme sniffed.

He drew her into his arms, quite alarmed by her behavior. "I don't give a damn about anything but you. I don't care what you said before or why you left. You are the most vexing, frustrating, exciting woman I've ever known. I love you with all my heart and soul. Marry me. Please, Esme. I don't want to lose you again."

If he had imagined Esme would accept him immediately, he was bound to be disappointed. She didn't utter a word.

He gently set his hands over her shoulders. "I will camp outside your door, follow you everywhere like a pathetic, lovelorn fool. I cannot pretend I don't care for you as much as I do. Berate me, scold me all you like, but I'm here and I'm not leaving without my wife."

Irritated beyond belief by her continued silence, he raised her face to his. Tears streaked down her cheeks as she silently wept.

Damn it, that wasn't the response he'd been hoping for

when he'd confessed how she'd changed him. He hadn't meant to upset her. He'd come to win her over and make her his own once and for all.

Richard crushed her against him. "Don't cry."

She burst out in loud, fresh sobs. "I cry at everything."

"Oh," he whispered, uncertain if that boded good or ill for their future. He'd never known her to shed a single tear, real or pretend, until their last night together. It was one of the many things he'd liked about her. She did not resort to sentimental theatrics to get her way. This new Esme, his soon-to-be wife and future mother of his child, would undoubtedly take some getting used to.

As he held her, peace settled over him. He could be reasonable. Wasn't Esme worth any sacrifice? "Well, continue if you like. I'm sure I can grow used to it."

Her sobbing renewed in strength and she buried her face against his neckcloth. She clutched his waistcoat and because it was Esme, and he was in love with the woman, he held her against him tightly and left her to it.

When she quieted, he moved a hand to touch her belly again. The knowledge Esme would bear his child gave him so much satisfaction he couldn't begin to describe it. He'd hoped but had never dared picture this day. A soft laugh left him. "You really were the one, the perfect woman for me all along."

She sniffed. "Well of course I'm the one. Who else could put up with you?"

He kissed the top of her head. He could see a happy life ahead, but not always a peaceful one. "Who else indeed? I promise you will have ample opportunity to test that theory. We will mold our children into strong-minded individuals who will never suffer fools. Our progeny will have every advantage in life and we will love them with our whole hearts, as we love each other, because we will tell them every day just how much of a miracle they are."

She sniffed again and glanced up. Despite looking at

him with glassy bright eyes, Esme had never been more beautiful to him. "Why are you so certain?"

"That I love you?" He touched his chest. "I feel it here, every time I think of our days together, every time I recall being told you'd already left my home without a word of farewell and left me with a list of potential wives to consider as replacements. I have ached to hold you against me, talk to you, every moment since you left me. I am so sorry. I should have followed you. If I had, you would never have had to be worried about the babe on your own. I would have reassured you that no matter what happens, I would always be in love with you."

Richard smiled gently. "I might not always make the right decisions for myself, but you'll have to grow accustomed to me knowing you better than you think. The list was a grave mistake."

She laughed a little. "I think so too."

He kissed her then, passionately and with all the longing he'd tried to contain for the past months without her in his life. He held nothing back in showing her how much he'd missed her. He was still as wild for her as their last night together in the woods.

He led her back to the chaise lounge and, with her permission this time, lifted her skirts to see her belly. The slender body and flat stomach he'd admired months ago was even more beautiful when rounded. As he stroked her skin, his breath caught as the child beneath his fingers moved as if drawn to his touch. "We will have smart children."

"Please do not get ahead of yourself," she chided. "One child is all I have ever hoped for. Don't expect more than this. Please. I couldn't bear to disappoint you."

"Oh, there will be more, I assure you." The wishing tree had wrought miracles. He leaned close to kiss her belly then let his hands slide lower over her thighs. "The moment I saw you today, I wanted to make love to you.

Desperately. We were meant for each other. I've felt this way every time you've left my arms."

Her fingers curled under his chin and she lifted his face to hers, delaying his wish to give her every imaginable pleasure with his tongue and mouth. "And I feel the same for you. It is the most disconcerting feeling. We have been enemies for so long."

He stood and rubbed his nose against hers. "Friendly enemies, clever girl. I have never hated you, even when you were giving me a proper set down."

She laughed then. "I will have to learn to curb my tongue as you must learn to heed my suggestions. Some of them. Most of them."

"I will try if you will. You'll of course share my bed most nights of our marriage." He winced at how pompous that sounded. "I am sure you believe that's another example of my arrogance, but it is going to be an absolute necessity you must accept here and now."

"Why is that?" She frowned.

He pressed his head to hers. "I'm liable to come looking for you in my sleep. You have no idea the difficulties my staff have faced in keeping me contained these past months. Being woken by a bucket of very cold water thrown in my face, in the middle of the night, halfway to the stables because my sleeping self has discovered how to pick a common lock, is not something I care to repeat too often."

"That must have been embarrassing." Her eyes widened. "Do you realize you never so much as twitched in sleep when we shared a bed?"

"Well, I had what I wanted most within reach then. Why would I wander when I had you in my arms?" He brushed his fingers over her cheek, loving her even more than he thought possible. "Now, onward to important matters. Can we make love today? I have no notion of how things must be done with a woman in your condition."

"Much the same, I'm told." She laughed suddenly. "So, there is to be no further discussion of our marriage? You just expect me to comply with your demands?"

Richard left Esme and locked the door for privacy. As he returned, he stripped himself of his jacket, waistcoat, cravat, and pulled his shirt over his head. Hearing Esme's moan of appreciation for the view of his skin made him happier still. He tossed everything aside carelessly and covered Esme as she slithered into a more comfortable position. He kept his weight suspended lest he crush her. "No demands but that you marry me, and as soon as possible please. I have learned my lesson. The only thing I know for certain anymore is that you're the one I want. The rest I leave to you to manage."

Esme burst out laughing and twined her arms about his neck, holding him firmly against a body he ached to feel bare against his once more. "I never intended to be the one you married," she confessed. "But I've not even felt desire for another man since our last night together."

"It's that blasted tree," he complained. "Turns a man into a lapdog and women into willing puppets."

"It wasn't the tree," she whispered. "It was the way you wanted me. I loved that. I love *you*."

He grinned at her words.

"Now for the last piece of the puzzle," she asked. "Did you hate tying me up?"

"Absolutely. I won't ever do it again." He grinned, remembering that night in the woods. "I like your hands on me too. And I'll have you know I have kept to your rules. I've considered myself a married man since your ravishment at the base of the wishing tree. I have been entirely faithful, both in thought and in deed, since our first kiss."

"Just as well." Her lips turned up at the corners. "I won't share you with anyone."

"You will never have to." He bent his head and licked

the plump swell of her lower lip before indulging in a leisurely kiss that made them both very restless on the chaise. "You are the only woman I want in my life and my bed. You'd better get used to being adored."

Esme's smile widened, her eyes filling with new tears. But they were tears of joy this time. And of happiness, he hoped. "Oh, I think I can accept that as my due. But you'll have to be very thorough, indeed, to reassure me in my delicate condition."

He framed her face with both hands. His joy was barely contained. Emotion clogged his throat and when he spoke next, his voice was a rough whisper. "Trust me, I have nothing else on my mind, awake or sleeping, other than you. My one and only love, forevermore."

Epilogue

———◆———

"Richard," Esme Hill, Countess of Windermere, bellowed at the top of her lungs. "Where have you taken our son?"

Richard launched to his feet and stared at his wife in shock as she appeared in the library doorway. "Good God, woman, you've just given birth. What are you doing out of bed?"

"I feel fine and the birth was yesterday." She glanced around the room. "So where is he?"

After their first child's rocky beginning, motherhood had come easily to Esme. It was a relief and a little alarming *how* well, actually. He'd hoped for an heir—just one son to carry on the Hill legacy and prevent the title from passing to his nosey cousin. He'd received far more than he'd bargained for with Esme as his wife.

"Hiding." He sank back down, knowing there were certain things he could argue with Esme about and other things that were not worth drawing breath for. Her health after laboring to deliver their children being one topic she refused to discuss with him. Ever. "I'm not to look for him until the clock strikes the hour."

She set her hands to her hips and glared. "I expect him to be returned to the nursery in the next half hour. He's to take a bath and that's final."

"Yes, my dear." He tilted his head to the side and smiled at his wife. God, she was lovely when she was annoyed with him. Six years married and he was still in love with the most fascinating woman he'd ever met. And desirable. He had weeks of abstinence ahead and then he could make love to her again. He hated waiting. "I love you, clever girl."

She scowled. "I love you too; just don't think seductive smiles like that are enough to appease me today. Your son has a woodsy odor about him from this morning's play outside."

He grinned. "He has to learn everything if he's to run this place once day. Mucking out the stables didn't hurt him. That's what my father did to me too. I turned out all right, didn't I?"

She huffed. "You did, eventually."

When she went on her way, he peeked under the table next to him and into two pairs of soft-blue eyes. "That was close, poppets. Mama didn't know I'd abducted you too, or I'd be in double trouble."

His two-year-old daughter Katie and four-year-old daughter Marie crawled from cover on hands and knees and then climbed onto his lap.

"Baby," the youngest cooed happily.

He smoothed her hair and winced when he found a piece of straw in the blonde locks. No doubt from the game she and Marie had played among the fresh hay. Katie might be in need of a bath too before her mother saw her again, and was that a smudge of earth on Marie's knee? He was going to pay for that later. "Yes, you'll have a little brother to play with soon. Baby Alistair just needs to grow a bit, so we must be quiet together while we wait until he's bigger."

Marie leaned into his chest, but then stretched to pull her sister's thumb from the girl's mouth. "I want to hold him again."

Not a request but a demand. Marie was so like Esme in

some respects that he grinned. "I'll see what I can do."

"And me too." Six-year-old Robert poked his head out of the cupboard he'd been hiding in, joining in with the idea. "Since Mama isn't resting anymore, can we go and see our new brother?"

"Can you be quiet as little mice?"

They all nodded.

"Can you not tell Mama about it later?"

They shook their heads and appeared sad about that fact that no matter what they promised, one stern look from their mother had them confessing to anything and everything.

He laughed. "Probably for the best."

A movement at the door caught his eye and when he looked in that direction, he discovered Esme standing there, watching him and their children plot against her. She shook her head, soft-blue eyes brimming with laughter.

"Always one step ahead of me," he complained.

"Someone has to be," she answered back immediately, looking extremely amused.

He stood, taking Katie into his arms and holding out his hand to Marie, and addressed the children. "Never does pay to keep anything from Mama because she'll always find out what we're up to. Come, it's time for your baths and then we'll make Mama take us to see Alistair so we don't all get in trouble, should we wake the baby."

He led them toward Esme, arms and heart full of love. He kissed his wife because he never could tire of showing her how much he adored her. He had a family he cherished to be sure, but only because one woman had made his life complete and had found a compelling enough reason to wed him in the end—love.

———◆———

The Trouble with Love

Keeping a promise has never been harder!

Whitney Crewe has a dream for her life, and it does not include a properly boring marriage or remaining in England. Passionate by nature, she's headed for an adventure abroad but has been temporarily lured into the countryside to paint an important family portrait. Unfortunately, a friend is set to marry the family's nearest neighbor, Lord Acton, and he is someone Whitney has seen far too much of...with and without his breeches on. Their past must remain a mere memory, but ignoring him proves impossible when she understands the decisions he's made to protect those he loves.

Lord Acton is keeping secrets from his friends, and particularly from his innocent bride-to-be. The first was losing his head over an intoxicating, veiled seductress one gloriously reckless evening. A man of his word, he has no choice but to keep his promise to wed, even after he discovers his seductress was his bride's friend, eccentric heiress and artist, Whitney Crewe. The second secret, Whitney stumbles upon all on her own, but her anger swiftly becomes an offer of friendship and much-needed compassion. They have absolutely nothing in common, so why oh why would he risk his future getting to know Whitney when she's opposed to everything he desires?

Prologue

London
March, 1814

Making merry didn't come easily for Everett Dean. The Earl of Acton did his duty, even if the weight of responsibility threatened to choke him at times. He sipped champagne slowly, casting an admiring glance over the lovely ladies who glided past his spot in the avenue of tall birch trees as if he'd not a care in the world.

Those who'd come to enjoy the Fairmont Bachelors Ball on the grounds of the expansive Fairmont estate were having a marvelous time without his participation. He could probably ask any one of the ladies to dance with him, but he did not want to give rise to unreasonable expectations beyond this one night.

Tomorrow it would be whispered that he was finally surveying the marriage mart and that could not be avoided. Those rumors would be true, if a little late. Everett had already chosen his bride, so he was uncertain why he'd felt a keen need to come to this unholy revel alone.

When he'd left his home, he'd originally had no intention of directing his driver to this spectacle but here he was, watching other people enjoy themselves. His hosts were not considered good *ton*. Lord and Lady Fairmont were more than a little eccentric in their habits, and in the company they kept. Within the manor behind him had been gathered mystics and fortune-tellers, determined to predict his future in exchange for coin. He'd pressed through their number without partaking or being taken for a fool. Acton did not need a fortune-teller to determine what his future path would bring. His future was already determined.

He would take a bride within the next month and that was that.

Miss Alice Quartermane was a fine choice for him. She was not in attendance tonight; she was not out in society yet, and her parents would certainly have shielded her gentle soul from boisterous depravity such as this. He had negotiated the marriage contract with her father last year while riding to hounds at a friend's estate, and he was looking forward to meeting Alice tomorrow in quieter surroundings at last.

Everett accepted another glass of champagne from a passing waiter and looked along the avenue of trees. He would not dance tonight out of respect for Alice, and would dissuade any damsel who might encourage him. Pretty women were in general a distraction from the serious business of being the head of a well-known and respected family. That was why he'd chosen the innocent Miss Alice Quartermane to be his wife. Her father knew his interests. They both agreed that Alice would be the perfect woman to become mistress of Warstone Manor, and his countess. It was the best possible arrangement for all concerned.

A flash of long bright red hair weaving through the trees ahead caught his eye. There were others following her, men and women making the most of the moonlit evening to dance gaily.

Everett was drawn toward them too, and smiling widely.

He'd lost his innocence to a redhead in Leeds at fifteen, been caught rutting with a russet-haired maid at eighteen, and after one final indignity—falling head over heels for a married countess—he wisely chose to keep his amours confined to fair-headed damsels ever since.

Miss Alice Quartermane was reputed to be blessed with very fair hair.

The redheaded woman was garbed as a gypsy—a prosperous lady, judging by the silk caressing her curves and the gold glittering on every finger under the torchlights as she weaved between the tree trunks. Her thumbs sparkled with gold bands too but her face was veiled, so all he could see were a pair of laughing, merry eyes.

But he felt her exuberant laughter as if she was stroking her jeweled fingers over his skin. She broke from the trees onto the clipped lawn and Everett followed. She lifted her skirts a little as she danced with careless abandon, revealing slender ankles and bare feet gliding upon the neatly trimmed lawns.

He drew closer, intrigued by the way she moved with unhindered sensuality. It was as if the darkness was her natural element, and she a flame in the midst of the chaos around her. She did not seem to care, or notice, that she was making a spectacle of herself.

He wasn't the only person who admired this woman. She continued to draw a crowd of admirers, even among the fairer sex. People stared, smiled at her transparent energy, and made a game of trying to copy her movements with varying degrees of success.

Everett was utterly entranced, and found a spot to watch as the redhead suddenly grabbed a lady, swinging her into her wild dance. They laughed in giddy joy, and soon the entire crowd was swaying to a beat that Everett had never seen before at a ton event.

The energy was compelling, the sounds and movements drawing him ever closer to the mass of humanity. He found himself surrounded, touched by strangers as they spun about on their merry way.

The redhead paused in her mad flight right in front of him and looked him directly in the eye as she had no one else so far. He acknowledged her with a dip of his head, unsure of what else he should do. He had not meant to curb her dancing. He'd been enjoying watching her sensual movements too much to desire that, but he was glad she had stopped.

He did not recognize her in the half dark but wanted to know her.

She held out her hand to him, fingers wriggling in invitation. The gems winked and he stepped forward.

Redheads were his weakness, but he suddenly didn't care one whit for caution or restraint or propriety. He took her bare fingers in his firmly. Her skin was soft and warm within his grasp and he didn't want to let go.

She tugged, and he followed her away from the crowds and into the house where it was quieter.

Their fingers still entwined, the lady led him toward a drinks table without a word, hips gently swaying ahead of him. She requested punch from a footman as she lowered her gauze veil.

"Dancing is thirsty work," she apologized in a husky tone between sips of her drink. "Why did you not join in and dance with us?"

He requested another beverage for the lady when she finished the first, trying to better see her face in the candlelight. She looked young, and very, very pretty to his eye. "How do you know I didn't dance?"

Her pretty green eyes glowed with delight. "Because I was watching you watching everyone else at play since you arrived in the garden. You are too serious, sir. Did you not read your invitation? Guests were supposed to leave their cares at the door."

"Life cannot be all fun and games."

"I don't see why not," she insisted. "As long as you hold reasonable expectations, it does not have to be full of misery. A little fun never hurt anyone."

"Is that so?"

The lady, having quenched her thirst, reset her veil over her face. "Indeed. Come with me."

She caught his hand again and pulled him along in her wake and into a deserted long gallery. Holding his hand firmly, she studied the paintings of their hosts' ancestors. "Look at this. You can tell just by looking at them that living life to the fullest extent was their goal. Don't you want a similar happiness for your own life?"

Everett gave the paintings a second longer glance, noting the couple closest to him were surrounded by hens and other farmyard fowl. "It is widely acknowledged that the Fairmont family possess a great number of eccentrics."

"I like eccentrics," she told him. "In fact, I have become one already. I will never do what is expected of me by society no matter how many long noses, and disapproving looks, bear down upon me."

His lips twitched in amusement. The woman had no idea of the trouble that attitude would cause her one day. "Already a rebel to propriety at your tender age."

"I am older than I appear to you, sir," she said, twirling a strand of red hair around one slender, bejeweled finger. "In my family, our looks change very slowly."

"Lucky you," he murmured. There was already streaks of gray in his hair at the temples and the odd strand at his crown. He felt time rushing past him—particularly so when he collected rents and saw how many men of his age had children old enough to work their farmland. But this woman had her whole life ahead of her. "Your hair has very distinct coloring."

"I'm wearing a wig," she confessed with a soft laugh.

It shocked him that she might really not be as she appeared tonight. He stretched out his hand and gathered a lock of her hair between his fingers. She felt real enough to him. "It's a very convincing wig."

Her brows were penciled, darkened with kohl, but he thought he detected a little bit of ginger underneath.

He lost his grip on her hair as the lady brushed her hair back over her shoulder. "Has anyone every told you that you are a very pretty fellow?"

Everett coughed in shock at the bold question. "Not to my face," he said, feeling his cheeks heat with embarrassment.

"But you are," she insisted. Her lips curved into a broad smile and she brushed her fingers across his cheek. She turned his face this way and that, studying him. "You have a face deserving serious consideration."

Her fingers were so firm and warm against his skin that he was astonished to feel himself become aroused just by her touch. "I would like to see more of your face, too."

The woman ignored his words as she traced each of his eyebrows, the shape of his nose, and again caressed his jawline, rasping her fingers against the grain of his new beard growth.

Her attention dropped to his lips, and he discovered he'd captured one between his teeth.

"Can I have you?" she asked.

He was flattered. A dalliance with the redhead wasn't wise, given his plans for tomorrow, but with her fingers still caressing his skin, his reasons for resistance began to erode. What could it hurt, this one last night to taste temptation before he became a properly devoted husband? "For tonight, but no more than that."

Her fingers slipped around his face to trace the edge of his ear. "But I could spend many days and nights studying this face." Her lips parted slightly.

She could not have more than this one night to know him, so he grabbed her hips firmly and tugged her close. "Only tonight."

She stood inches under his height of six feet three, slender but utterly feminine in silk. Her body was so soft and warm as she pressed against him. She burrowed her nose against his neck and inhaled as her arms slipped under his coat. Her hungry moan shocked him because it matched the way he was feeling.

Everett had some idea of the layout of the Fairmont estate, so he propelled the woman into a nearby chamber before anyone came along to interrupt them and closed the door.

"What is your name?"

"My friends call me Trouble," she whispered. "Undress for me."

It bothered him only a moment that she did not ask for his name before he removed his coat and kicked off his shoes. "Not completely."

She drew back, her eyes narrowing on his lower half. "Then please remove the clothing that is in the way of what I want to see."

It was hard to miss her meaning when her attention dropped to the region of his hips and the erection he should be hiding. He wasn't usually so easily aroused, but he put his hands to the waistband of his breeches and slipped the buttons free. He pushed his shirt up and lowered his smallclothes to reveal his cock. "Is this what you want?"

She purred, coming closer before she wrapped her fingers around him. Everett hissed at the sensation of her hand on him. He couldn't help but thrust his hips forward as she proved her experience without a doubt or hint of shyness.

"Remove your veil," he whispered.

"Why is it that you are alone?" she whispered back without complying.

He covered her hand and slowed down her strokes, trying to see past the veil to learn more of her identity. "I'm not alone now."

Everett lifted the veil a little and leaned forward to deliver a kiss to her cheek, but the woman jerked back, her fingers catching on his clothing momentarily.

The woman clucked her tongue and resettled the rings on her fingers. "Kissing is for romantics."

"Most women enjoy kisses."

"I'm not most women," she promised him.

"I see that." Cautious of scaring her off again, he brought her hand back to his cock and closed her fingers around him. "So you are not romantic *at all?*"

"I am the furthest thing from it as a woman my age can be." She resumed stroking him firmly. "I am practical. I give and take my pleasures where I can, without any hesitation or regret, sir. I have no need for a husband or protector, but I do desire being with pretty men from time to time. You interest me tonight, and I want you."

"I'm flattered."

She clenched the top of his cock and held still. "Stolen moments of pleasure bring meaning to my life. A quick dalliance can satisfy far better than a drawn-out love affair can, and with far less trouble. Do you agree to my terms?"

She squeezed him a little harder, and he groaned when her hand slid down his length again and clenched him at the base. "Yes."

He let the veiled woman have her way, quite frankly because he was utterly under her spell. He'd never known a woman to speak so boldly of pleasure on first making his acquaintance. He'd never inspired such passion before, and her focus on him went to his head.

She stroked him almost to the brink of completion then stopped. "Take off your breaches and the rest of your clothes. They are in the way of what I want now."

Feeling a little desperate for her to continue, Everett stepped back, stripped off his waistcoat and shirt, and everything else he was wearing until he stood nude in the room. He let everything fall to the parquetry floor but heard a button or such bounce away. He couldn't care where it landed right now. He wasn't one for unguarded romps, but this woman, Trouble, had him twisted around her dainty bejeweled fingers. "Satisfied, madam?"

"That's better. Now I can determine that all of you deserves to be worshiped. The real you is exquisite, rather than the carefully constructed society gentleman keeping himself apart from happiness." She took a pace toward him, her glance admiring and decidedly hungry. She unwound the fringed shawl she'd tied about her waist and dropped it onto his clothing. "This moment is when lovers are the most raw, most vulnerable. I must have you."

"Honestly, I think I must be had," he said with a strangled laugh as she returned and took him in hand again, torturing him with lazy strokes. He caught her hips, kneading her curves and considered having her against the wall if she was agreeable. "By you, and all night," he agreed.

The woman cupped his ballocks, kneading him carefully with one hand, but he still moaned. She traced the muscles of his back with her other hand and then cupped the back of his neck. "Lovely," she whispered. "I'm so glad we met tonight. This is an auspicious beginning."

He was glad he'd come tonight too, but... "I'm to be married soon," he cautioned her.

The woman released him so suddenly he cursed out loud.

"Married? When?" she demanded.

"Just as soon as I meet the woman." He said it with a laugh but his companion did not join in.

"You... You are engaged to be married without ever meeting her first?"

He nodded, puzzled by her outrage. "Yes, that's the way it's always been done in my family—for generations."

"Sir, this is a bachelors ball. Hen-pecked husbands and panicking engaged men were not invited." She bent to snatch up her shawl from the parquetry floor and hugged it to her chest. "I thought you knew the rules for this evening's revel."

"We were hardly doing anything out of the ordinary, and I am not engaged yet."

"Merely intending to be so from tomorrow?" Her gaze hardened, but then she rolled her eyes. "And people wonder why I'm opposed to marriage. An arranged match? I suppose she comes from a wealthy family too and has only just come out?"

"She's not out yet," he confessed, feeling just a touch defensive on the subject. "The money from her dowry wasn't why I chose her, but it is vital for the future of my estate and our children."

"Fortune hunter!" She nearly shouted. "No wonder you look so sad, but I will not pity you. I pity the poor child, married before she's even had a chance to enjoy her first season and a little attention."

"Now just a minute," he protested. "I'm not going to marry the chit tomorrow."

The woman advanced on him, stabbing him in the chest with her finger. "You, sir, should really consider if this arranged marriage is what you want before it is too late to remove the scowl you wear when you speak of it. Goodbye."

"Wait!"

"For you?" She looked him up and down coldly and then shook her head. "I'd rather drink paint."

More Regency Romance from Heather Boyd...

Saints and Sinners Series

Book 1: The Duke and I
Book 2: A Gentleman's Vow
Book 3: An Earl of Her Own

Rebel Hearts Series

Book 1: The Wedding Affair
Book 2: An Affair of Honor
Book 3: The Christmas Affair
Book 4: An Affair so Right

The Wild Randalls Series

Book 1: Engaging the Enemy
Book 2: Forsaking the Prize
Book 3: Guarding the Spoils
Book 4: Hunting the Hero

Miss Mayhem Series

Book 1: Miss Watson's First Scandal
Book 2: Miss George's Second Chance
Book 3: Miss Radley's Third Dare
Book 4: Miss Merton's Last Hope

And many more...

About Heather Boyd

Determined to escape the Aussie sun on a scorching camping holiday, Heather picked up a pen and notebook from a corner store and started writing her very first novel—Chills. Years later, she is the author of over thirty sexy regency historical romances. Addicted to all things tech (never again will Heather write a novel longhand) and fascinated by English society of the early 1800's, Heather spends her days getting her characters in and out of trouble and into bed together (if they make it that far). She lives on the edge of beautiful Lake Macquarie, Australia with her trio of mischievous rogues (husband and two sons) along with one rescued cat whose only interest in her career is that it provides him with food on demand and a new puppy that is proving a big distraction.

You can find details of her work and writing at
www.Heather-Boyd.com